THE SCARECROW AND HIS SERVANT

One night a fierce thunderstorm raged over the countryside. A tattered scarecrow stood in the wind and rain, taking no notice—until a bolt of lightning struck his turnip head. The scarecrow blinked with surprise and came to life. So begins the story of the Scarecrow, a courteous but pea-brained fellow with grand ideas. He meets a boy, Jack, who becomes his faithful servant. Leaving behind his usual bird-scaring duties, the Scarecrow sets out for Spring Valley, with Jack at his side. Along the way there's no end of excitement, not least avoiding the many members of the crooked Buffaloni family. As the valiant scarecrow plunges them into terrifying dangers—pirates and treasure islands, brigands and broken hearts—it's up to Jack to save the day.

THE SCARECROW AND HIS SERVANT

Philip Pullman

Illustrated by Peter Bailey

First published in 2004
by
Doubleday
This Large Print edition published by
BBC Audiobooks Ltd
by arrangement with
Random House Children's Books
2005

ISBN 1 4056 6031 7

Text copyright © Philip Pullman, 2004
Illustrations copyright © Peter Bailey, 2004
Philip Pullman raven illustration by
John Lawrence.

British Library Cataloguing in Publication Data available

Printed and bound in Great Britain by
Antony Rowe Ltd., Chippenham, Wiltshire

For Freddie

CHAPTER ONE

LIGHTNING

One day old Mr Pandolfo, who hadn't been feeling at all well, decided that it was time to make a scarecrow. The birds had been very troublesome. Come to that, his rheumatism had been troublesome, and the soldiers had been troublesome, and the weather had been troublesome, and his cousins had been troublesome. It was all getting a bit too much for him. Even his old pet raven had flown away.

He couldn't do anything about his rheumatism, or the soldiers, or the weather, or his cousins, who were the biggest problem of all. There was a whole family of them, the Buffalonis, and they wanted to get hold of his land and divert all the springs and streams, and drain all the wells, and put up a factory to make weedkiller and rat poison and insecticide.

All those troubles were too big for old Mr Pandolfo to manage, but he thought he could do something about the birds, at least. So he put together a fine-looking scarecrow, with a big solid turnip for a head and a sturdy broomstick for a backbone, and dressed him in an old tweed suit, and stuffed him tightly with straw. Then he tucked a short letter inside him, wrapped in oilskin for safety.

'There you are,' he said. 'Now you remember what your job is, and remember where you belong. Be courteous, and be brave, and be honourable, and be kind. And the best of blooming luck.'

He stuck the scarecrow in the middle of the wheatfield, and went home to lie down, because he wasn't feeling well at all.

That night another farmer came along and stole the scarecrow, being too lazy to make one himself. And the next night someone else came along and stole him again.

So little by little the scarecrow moved away from the place where he was made, and he got more and more tattered and torn, and finally he didn't look nearly as smart as he'd done when Mr Pandolfo put him together. He stood in the middle of a muddy field, and he stayed there.

But one night there was a thunderstorm. It was a very violent one, and everyone in the district shivered and trembled and jumped as the thunder went off like cannon-fire and the lightning lashed down like whips. The scarecrow stood there in the wind and the rain, taking no notice.

And so he might have stayed; but then there came one of those million-to-one chances that are like winning the lottery. All his molecules and atoms and elementary particles and whatnot were lined up in exactly the right way to switch on when the lightning struck him, which it did at two in the morning, fizzing its way through his turnip and down his broomstick and into the mud.

The Scarecrow blinked with surprise and looked all around. There wasn't much to see except a field of mud, and not much light to see it by except the flashes of lightning.

Still, there wasn't a bird in sight.

'Excellent,' said the Scarecrow.

On the same night, a small boy called Jack happened to be sheltering in a barn not far away. The thunder was so loud that it woke him out of his sleep with a jump. At first he thought it was cannon-fire, and he sat up terrified with his eyes wide open. He could think of nothing worse than soldiers and guns; if it weren't for the soldiers, he'd still have a family and a home and a bed to sleep in.

But as he sat there with his heart thumping, he heard the downpour of the rain on the roof, and realized that the bang had only been thunder and not gunfire. He gave a sigh of relief and lay down again, shivering and sneezing and turning over and over in the hay trying to get warm, until finally he fell asleep.

By the morning the storm had cleared away, and the sky was a bright cold blue. Jack woke up again feeling colder than ever, and hungry too. But he knew how to look for food, and before long he'd

3

gathered up some grains of wheat and a couple of turnip tops and a limp carrot, and he sat in the doorway of the barn in the sunlight to eat them.

'Could be worse,' he said to himself.

He ate very slowly to make it last, and then he just sat there, getting warm. Someone would come along soon to chase him away, but for the moment he was safe.

Then he heard a voice calling from across the fields. Jack was curious, so he stood up and shaded his eyes to look. The shouting came from somewhere in the field beyond the road, and since he had nothing else to do, Jack stood up and walked along towards it.

The shouts came from a scarecrow, in the middle of the muddiest field in sight, and he was waving his arms wildly and yelling at the top of his voice and leaning over at a crazy angle.

'Help!' he was shouting. 'Come and help me!'

'I think I'm going mad,' said Jack to himself. 'Still, look at that poor old thing—I'll go and help him anyway. He looks madder than I feel.'

So he stepped on to the muddy field, and struggled out to the middle, where the Scarecrow was waiting.

To tell the truth, Jack felt a little nervous, because it isn't every day you find a Scarecrow talking to you.

'Now, tell me, young man,' said the Scarecrow, as soon as Jack was close enough to hear, 'are there any birds around? Any crows, for example? I can't see behind me. Are they hiding?'

His voice was rich and sonorous. His head was made of a great knobbly turnip, with a broad crack for a mouth and a long thin sprout for a nose and

4

two bright little stones for eyes. He had a tattered straw hat, now badly singed, and a soggy woollen scarf, and an old tweed jacket full of holes, and his rake-handle arms had gloves stuffed with straw on the ends of them, one glove leather and the other wool. He also had a pair of threadbare trousers, but since he only had one leg, the empty trouser leg trailed down beside him. Everything was the colour of mud. Jack scratched his head and looked all around.

'No,' he said, 'no crows anywhere. No birds at all.'

'That's a good job done,' said the Scarecrow. 'Now I want to move on, but I need another leg. If you go and find me a leg, I shall be very obliged. Just like this one, only the opposite,' he added, and he lifted his trouser leg daintily to show a stout stick set firmly in the earth.

'All right,' said Jack. 'I can do that.'

So he set off towards the wood at the edge of the field, and clambered through the undergrowth looking for the right sort of stick. He found one before long, and took it back to the Scarecrow.

'Let me see,' said the Scarecrow. 'Hold it up beside me. That's it. Now slide it up inside the leg of my trousers.'

The end of the stick was broken and splintered and it wasn't easy to push it up the soggy, muddy trouser leg, but Jack finally got it all the way up, and then he jumped, because he felt it twitch in his hand.

He let go, and the new leg swung itself down beside the other. But as soon as the Scarecrow tried to move, the new foot became stuck just like the first one. The harder he struggled, the deeper

5

he sank.

Finally he stopped, and looked at Jack. It was astonishing how much expression he could manage with his gash-mouth and stone-eyes.

'Young man,' he said, 'I have a proposition to make. Here you are, an honest and willing youth, and here am I, a Scarecrow of enterprise and talent. What would you say if I offered you the position of my personal servant?'

'What would my duties be?' said Jack.

'To accompany me throughout the world, to fetch and carry, to wash, cook, and attend to my needs. In return, I have nothing to offer but excitement and glory. We might sometimes go hungry, but we shall never want for adventure. Well, my boy? What do you say?'

'I'll do it,' said Jack. 'I've got nothing else to do except starve, and nowhere to live except ditches and empty barns. So I might as well have a job, and thank you, Mr Scarecrow, I'll take it.'

The Scarecrow extended his hand, and Jack shook it warmly.

'Your first job is to get me out of this mud,' said the Scarecrow.

So Jack heaved the Scarecrow's two legs out of the mud and carried him to the road. He hardly weighed anything at all.

'Which way shall we go?' said Jack.

They looked both ways. In one direction there was a forest, and in the other there was a line of hills. There was no-one in sight.

'That way!' said the Scarecrow, pointing to the hills.

So they set off, with the sun on their backs, and the green hills ahead.

6

*   *   *

In a farmhouse not far behind them, a lawyer was explaining something to a farmer.

'My name is Cercorelli,' he said, 'and I specialize in finding things for my employers, the distinguished and highly respectful Buffaloni Corporation, of Bella Fontana.'

The farmer gasped. He was a stout, red-faced, idle character, and he was afraid of this lean and silky lawyer, who was dressed entirely in black.

'Oh! The Buffalonis! Yes, indeed, Mr Cercorelli,' he said. 'What can I do to help? Anything! Just name it!'

'It's a small matter,' said the lawyer, 'but one of sentimental importance to my clients. It concerns a scarecrow. It was made by a distant cousin of the Chairman of the Corporation, and it seems to have vanished from its place of origin. My client Mr Giovanni Buffaloni is a very warm-hearted and family-minded man, and he would like to restore the scarecrow to its original home, in memory of his dear cousin who made it.'

The lawyer looked through some papers, and the farmer ran his finger around the inside of his shirt collar, and gulped.

'Well, I, um . . .' he said faintly.

'One might almost think that scarecrows had the power of movement!' said Mr Cercorelli, smiling in a sinister way. 'This fellow has been wandering. I've traced him through several farms already, and now I discover that he made his way to yours.'

'I—er—I think I know the scarecrow you mention,' said the farmer. 'I nick— I bought him

8

from someone else, who didn't need him no more.'

'Oh, good. May we go and see if he is the right one?'

'Well, of course, I'd do anything for the Buffalonis, important people, wouldn't want to upset them, but . . . Well, he's gone.'

'Gone . . . *again*?' said the lawyer, narrowing his eyes.

'I went out this morning, to—er—to tidy him up a bit, and he wasn't there. Mind you, there was a big storm last night. He might have blown away.'

'Oh, dear. That is very unfortunate. Mr Buffaloni takes a dim view of people who do not look after his property. I think I can say that his degree of disappointment will be considerable.'

The farmer was quaking with alarm.

'If I ever hear anything about the scarecrow,' he said, 'anything at all, I'll report to you at once.'

'I think that would be very wise,' said Mr Cercorelli. 'Here is my card. Now show me the field from which the scarecrow vanished.'

CHAPTER TWO

THE BRIGANDS

The Scarecrow and his servant set a good pace as they walked along. On the way, they passed a field of cabbages in the middle of which stood another scarecrow, but he was a mournful-looking fellow whose arms hung feebly at his side.

'Good day to you, sir!' called the Scarecrow, waving to him cheerfully.

But the scarecrow in the field took no notice.

'You see,' the Scarecrow explained to Jack, 'there's a man whose mind is on his job. He's concentrating hard. Quite right.'

'Nice-looking cabbages,' said Jack.

He left the cabbages reluctantly and ran to catch up with the Scarecrow, who was striding ahead like a champion. Presently they found the road getting steeper and the fields getting rockier, and finally there were no fields at all and the road was only a track. It was very hot.

'Unless we find something to eat and drink very soon,' said Jack, 'I'm going to peg out.'

'Oh, we'll find something,' said the Scarecrow, patting him on the shoulder. 'I have every confidence in you. Besides, we understand springs and streams and wells where I come from. Fountains, too. You take it from me, we'll find a spring before long.'

They walked on, and the Scarecrow pointed out curious features of geology, such as a rock that looked like a pigeon, and botany, such as a bush with a robin's nest in it, and entomology, such as a beetle that was as black as a crow.

'You know a lot about birds, master,' said Jack.

'I've made them my lifetime study, my boy. I do believe I could scare any bird that ever lived.'

'I bet you could. Oh! Listen! What's that?'

It was the sound of someone crying, and it came from round the corner. Jack and the Scarecrow hurried on, and found an old woman sitting at a crossroads, with a basket of provisions all scattered on the ground. She was weeping and wailing at the top of her voice.

'Madam!' the Scarecrow said, raising his straw hat very politely. 'What wicked bird has done this to you?'

The old woman looked up, and gave a great gulp of astonishment. Her mouth opened and shut several times, but not a sound came out. Finally, she struggled to her feet and curtseyed nervously.

'It was the brigands,' she said, 'begging your pardon, my lord. There's a gang of terrible brigands living in these hills, robbing travellers and making life a misery for us poor people, and they just came galloping past and knocked me over and rode away laughing, the cowardly rogues.'

The Scarecrow was amazed.

'Do you mean to say that this was the work of *human beings*?' he said.

'Indeed, yes, your honour,' said the old woman.

'Jack, my boy—tell me it's not so—'

Jack was gathering up the things that had fallen out of her basket: apples, carrots, a lump of cheese, a loaf of bread. It was very difficult to do it without dribbling.

'I'm afraid it is, master,' said Jack. 'There's a lot of wicked people about. Tell you what—let's turn round and go the other way.'

'Not a bit of it!' said the Scarecrow sternly. 'We're going to teach these villains a lesson. How dare they treat a lady in this disgraceful way? Here, madam—take my arm . . .'

He was so courteous to the old woman, and his manner was so graceful, that she very soon forgot his knobbly turnip face and his rough wooden arms, and talked to him as if he was a proper gentleman.

'Yes, sir—ever since the wars began, first the soldiers came through and took everything, and then the brigands came along, robbing and murdering and taking what they wanted. And they say the chief brigand is related to the Buffalonis, so they've got political protection too. We don't know where to turn!'

'Buffalonis, you say? I don't like the sound of them. What are they?'

'A very powerful family, sir. We don't dare cross the Buffalonis.'

'Well, fear no more,' said the Scarecrow resolutely. 'We shall scare the brigands away, and they'll never trouble you again.'

'Nice-looking apples,' said Jack hopefully, handing the old woman her basket.

'Ooh, they are,' she said.

'Tasty-looking bread, too.'

'Yes, it is,' said the old woman, tucking it firmly under her arm.

'Lovely-looking cheese.'

'Yes, I like a piece of cheese. Goes down a treat with a drop of beer.'

'You haven't got any beer, have you?' said Jack, looking all around.

'No,' she said. 'Well, I'll be on my way. Thank you, sir,' she said, curtseying again to the Scarecrow, who raised his hat and bowed.

And off she went.

Jack sighed and followed the Scarecrow, who was already striding off towards the top of the hill.

When they reached the top, they saw a ruined

13

castle. There was one tower that was still standing, and some walls and battlements, but everything else had tumbled down and was covered in ivy.

'What a spooky place,' said Jack. 'I wouldn't like to go near it at night.'

'Courage, Jack!' said the Scarecrow. 'Look—there's a spring. What did I tell you? Drink your fill, my boy!'

It was true. The spring bubbled out of the rocks beside the castle and flowed into a little pool, and as soon as he saw it, Jack gave a cry of delight and plunged his face deep into the icy water, swallowing and swallowing until he wasn't thirsty any more.

Finally he emerged, and heard the Scarecrow calling.

'Jack! Jack! In here! Look!'

Jack ran through the doorway at the foot of the tower, and found the Scarecrow looking around at all kinds of things: in one corner, barrels of gunpowder, muskets, swords and daggers and pikes; and in another corner, chests and boxes of gold coins and silver chains and glittering jewels of every colour; and in a third corner—

'Food!' cried Jack.

There were great smoked hams hanging from the ceiling, cheeses as big as cartwheels, onions in strings, boxes of apples, pies of every kind, bread, biscuits, and spice cakes and fruit cakes and butter cakes and honey cakes in abundance.

It was no good even trying to resist. Jack seized a pie as big as his own head, and a moment later he was sitting in the middle of the food, chewing away merrily, while the Scarecrow watched in satisfaction.

'What a stroke of luck finding this!' he said. 'And

14

no-one knows about it at all. If only that old lady knew about it, she could come and help herself, and she wouldn't be poor any more.'

'Well,' said Jack, swallowing a mouthful of pie and picking up a spice cake, 'it's not quite like that, master. I bet all this belongs to the brigands, and we better clear off soon, because if they catch us they'll cut our throats.'

'But I haven't got a throat.'

'Well, I have, and I don't want it cut,' said Jack. 'Look—we can't stay here—let's grab some of the food and scram.'

'Shame on you!' said the Scarecrow severely. 'Where's your courage? Where's your honour? We're going to scare these brigands away, and scare them so badly that they never come back. I wouldn't be surprised if we win a grand reward. Why, they might even make me a duke! Or give me a gold medal. No, it wouldn't surprise me a bit.'

'Well,' said Jack, 'maybe.'

Suddenly the Scarecrow pointed at a heap of straw.

'Oh—look—what's that?' he said.

There was something moving. It was a little creature the size of a mouse, which was crawling feebly around in a heap of straw on the floor. They both bent over to look at it.

'It's a baby bird,' said Jack.

'It's an owl chick, that's what it is,' said the Scarecrow severely. 'These parents have no sense of responsibility. Look at that nest up there! Downright dangerous.'

He pointed to an untidy bundle of twigs in a crack high up in the wall.

'Well, there's only one thing for it,' he said. 'You

15

keep guard, Jack, while I return this infant to his cradle.'

'But—' Jack tried to protest.

The Scarecrow took no notice. He bent over and picked up the little bird, and tucked it tenderly into his pocket, making gentle clucking noises to soothe it. Then he began to clamber perilously up the sheer face of the wall, jamming his hands and feet into the cracks.

'Master! Take care!' called Jack, in a fever of anxiety. 'If you fall down, you'll snap like a dry stick!'

The Scarecrow didn't listen, because he was concentrating hard. Jack scampered to the door and looked around. Darkness was gathering, but there was no sign of any brigands. He scampered back in, and saw the Scarecrow high up and clinging to the wall with one hand while fumbling in his pocket with the other, and then reaching up and carefully putting the little bird back into the nest.

'Now you sit still,' he said sternly. 'No more squirming, you understand? If you can't fly, don't squirm. When I see your parents, I shall have a word with them.'

Then he began to clamber back down the wall. It looked so dangerous that Jack hardly dared watch, but finally the Scarecrow reached the floor again, and brushed his hands severely.

'I thought the birds were your enemy, master,' said Jack.

'Not the children, Jack! Good gracious me. Any man of honour would sooner bite off his own leg than hurt a child. Heaven forfend!'

'Blimey,' said Jack.

While the Scarecrow pottered about in the ruins, looking at everything with great curiosity, Jack gathered up a couple of pies, a loaf of bread, and half a dozen apples, and put them in a leather bag he found hanging on a hook next to the muskets. He hid it among the ivy growing over the tumbled wall outside.

The sun had set by this time, and it was nearly dark. Jack sat on the stones and thought about brigands. What did they do to people they caught? They weren't like scarecrows, or men of honour; they were more like soldiers, probably. They were bound to do horrible things, like tying you up and cutting bits off you, or dangling you over a fire, or putting earwigs up your nose. They might take all your ribs out. They might cram your trousers full of fireworks. They might—

Someone tapped him on the shoulder, and Jack leaped up with a yell.

'My word,' said the Scarecrow admiringly, 'that's a fine noise. I was just going to tell you that the brigands are coming.'

'What?' said Jack, in terror.

'Come, come,' said the Scarecrow. 'It's only a small flock—not more than twenty, I'd say. And I've got a plan.'

'Let's hear it, quick!'

'Very well. Here it is: we'll hide in the castle until they're all inside, and then we'll scare them, and then they'll run away. How's that?'

Jack was speechless. The Scarecrow beamed.

'Come along,' he said. 'I've found an excellent place to hide.'

Helplessly, Jack followed his master back into the tower, and looked all around in the dimness.

18

'Where's this excellent place to hide?' he said.

'Why, over there!' said the Scarecrow, pointing to a corner of the room in plain sight. 'They'll never think of looking there.'

'But—but—but—'

Jack could already hear the clop of horses' hooves outside. He scrunched himself down in the corner beside the Scarecrow, and squeezed his knees together to stop them knocking, and put his hands over his eyes so that no-one could see him, and waited for the brigands to come in.

CHAPTER THREE

A STORY BY THE FIRESIDE

They were a disciplined band, those brigands. Jack watched between his fingers as they came in silently and sat around the fireplace. The chief brigand was a ferocious-looking man, with two belts full of bullets criss-cross over his shoulders, another one round his waist, a cutlass, two pistols, and three daggers: one in his belt, another strapped to his arm, and the third in the top of his boot. What's more, if he lost all his other weapons he could still stab two people with his moustache, which was waxed into long points as sharp as a pin.

His eyes glared and rolled as he looked around at his men, and Jack was almost sure they gave out sparks.

Any second now he'll see us, Jack thought. So it was despair as much as bravado that made him stand up and say:

'Good evening, gentlemen, and welcome to my

master's castle!'

And he swept a low bow.

When he looked around, he saw twenty swords and twenty pistols all pointing at him, and twenty pairs of eyes, each eye just like the end of a pistol barrel.

The chief brigand roared: 'Who's this?'

'It's a mad boy, Captain,' said one of the men. 'Shall we roast him?'

'No,' said the chief, coming close and touching Jack's ribs with the point of his sword. 'There's no meat on him. He's all bone and gristle. He might flavour a stew, I suppose. Turn round, boy.'

Jack turned round and then turned back again. The chief brigand was shaking his head doubtfully.

'You say this is your master's castle?' he said.

'Indeed it is, sir, and you're most welcome,' said Jack.

'And who's your master?'

'My Lord Scarecrow,' said Jack, pointing to the Scarecrow in the corner, who was lying propped against the wall as still as a turnip, a suit of old clothes, and a few sticks could lie.

The chief brigand roared with laughter, and all his well-trained band slapped their thighs and held their sides and bellowed with mirth.

21

'He is mad!' cried the chief brigand. 'He's lost his wits!'

'Indeed I have, sir,' said Jack. 'I've been looking for them for months.'

'What do mad boys taste like?' said one of the brigands. 'Do they taste different from normal ones?'

'Spicier,' said another. 'More of a peppery taste.'

'No!' said the chief. 'We won't eat him. We'll keep him as a pet. We'll teach him to do tricks. Here—mad boy—turn a somersault, go on.'

Jack turned a somersault and stood up again.

'He's quick, isn't he?' said one brigand.

'Bet he can't dance, though,' said another.

'Mad boy!' roared the chief. 'Dance!'

Jack obediently capered like a monkey. Then he capered like a frog, and then he capered like a goat. The brigands were in a good mood by now, and they roared with laughter and clapped their hands.

'Wine!' bellowed the chief. 'Mad boy, stop dancing and pour us some wine!'

Jack found a big flagon of wine and went around the circle of brigands, filling up the horn cups they were all holding out.

'A toast!' the chief brigand said. 'To plunder!'

'To plunder!' the brigands shouted, and drank the wine in one gulp, so Jack had to go all the way round and fill the cups again.

Meanwhile, some of the brigands were lighting a fire and cutting up great joints of meat. Jack looked at the meat uneasily, but it looked like proper beef, and it certainly smelled good when it started to cook.

While it was roasting, the chief brigand counted

out the jewels and gold coins they'd plundered and divided them all into twenty heaps, one big one and nineteen little ones; and as he was doing that, he said, 'Here, mad boy—tell us a story.'

Well, that was a hard one for Jack. However, if he didn't do it there'd be big trouble; so he sat down and began.

'Once upon a time,' he said, 'there was a band of brigands living in a cave. They were cruel and wicked—oh, you could never imagine such terrible men. Every one of them was a qualified murderer.

'Anyway, one day they fell to quarrelling among themselves, and before they knew it, one of them lay dead on the floor of the cave.

'So the chief said, "Take him out and bury him. He makes the place look untidy."

'And they picked the dead man up and took him outside and dug a hole for him, and they put him in and shovelled the earth back on top, but he kept throwing it out.

' "You're not burying me!" he said, and he climbed out of the grave.

' "Oh yes we are!" they said, and they tried to shove him back in, but he wouldn't go. Every time they got him in the grave, he climbed out again, and he was as dead as a doornail. Finally they got him in and seven of them sat on him while the others piled rocks on top, and that did it.

' "He won't get out of that," said the chief, and they went back in the cave and lit a fire to make supper. They had a big meal and lots of wine and then they lay down to sleep.

'But in the middle of the night, one of the brigands woke up. The cave was all silent, and the moonlight was shining in through the entrance.

What woke him up was a sound, like a rock moving quietly on another rock, not loud at all, just a quiet sort of scraping noise. This man lay there with his eyes wide open, just listening as hard as he could. Then he heard it again.'

All the brigands were sitting stock-still, and they gazed fearfully at Jack with wide eyes.

Help, he thought. What am I going to say next?

But he didn't have to say anything, because into the silence there came a little scraping sound, like a rock moving quietly on another rock.

All the brigands jumped, and they all gave a little squeak of terror.

'And then,' said Jack, 'he saw . . . *Look! Look!'*

And he pointed dramatically to the corner where the Scarecrow was lying. Every head turned round at once.

The Scarecrow slowly lifted his head and stared at them with his knobbly turnip face.

All the brigands gasped, including the chief.

And the Scarecrow stretched out his arms and bent his legs, and stood up, and took one step towards them—

And every single brigand leaped to his feet and fled, screaming with terror. They fell over—they knocked one another out of the way—the ones that fell over got trampled on, and the ones that trampled on them got their feet caught and fell over themselves, to be trampled on in their turn— and some of them fell in the fire and leaped up squealing with pain, and that scattered the burning logs so that the cave was dark, and that made them even more frightened, so they shrieked and yelled in mortal fear; and those who could still see a little saw the Scarecrow's great knobbly face coming

24

towards them, and scrambled even harder to get away—

And no more than ten seconds later, the brigands were all running away down the road, screaming with terror.

Jack stood in the doorway in amazement, watching them disappear into the distance.

'Well, master,' he said, 'it happened just as you said it would.'

'Timing, you see,' said the Scarecrow. 'The secret of all good scaring. I waited till they were feeling at their ease, lulled and comfortable, you know, and then I got up and scared them good and proper. It was the last thing they expected. I expect your story helped a little,' he added. 'It probably put them in a sort of peaceful mood.'

'Hmm,' said Jack. 'But I bet they come back, because they haven't eaten their dinner. I reckon we should scarper before they do.'

'Believe me,' said the Scarecrow solemnly, 'those rascals will never come back. They're not like birds, you see. With birds you need to keep scaring them afresh every day, but once is enough for brigands.'

'Well, you were right once, master. Perhaps you're right again.'

'You can depend on it, my boy! But you know, you shouldn't have told the brigands that I was the lord of this castle. That wasn't strictly true. I'm really the lord of Spring Valley.'

'Spring Valley? Where's that?'

'Oh, miles away. Ever so far. But it all belongs to me.'

'Does it?'

'Every inch. The farm, the wells, the fountains, the streams—all of it.'

'But how do you know, master? I mean, can you prove it?'

'The name of Spring Valley is written in my heart, Jack! Anyway, now I've had a rest, I'm eager to be on our way, and see the world by moonlight. Perhaps we'll meet the parents of that poor little owl chick. My word, I look forward to scaring them. Take as much food as you like—the brigands won't need it now.'

So Jack took the bag of food he'd hidden earlier, and added a pie and a cold roast chicken to it for good measure, and then followed his master out on to the high road, which was shining bright under the moon.

*   *   *

At that very moment, Mr Cercorelli the lawyer was sitting at a rough wooden table in a cottage kitchen, opposite an old woman who was eating bread and cheese.

'Like a scarecrow, you say?' he said, making a note.

'Yes, sir, horrible ugly brute he was. He leaped out of the bushes at me. Lord! I thought my last hour had come. He give me such a start that I dropped all me bread and cheese, and it was only when young master Buffaloni and his nice friends come along and chased him away that I felt safe again.'

'And did you see which way he went, this footpad who looked like a scarecrow?'

'Yes, sir. He went up into the hills. I shouldn't wonder if he's got a gang of marauding villains up there with him.'

27

'No doubt. Was he alone on this occasion?'

'No, sir. He had a young boy with him. Vicious-looking lad. Foreign, probably.'

'A young boy, eh?' said the lawyer, making another note. 'Thank you. That is very interesting. By the way,' he said, because he hadn't eaten all day, 'that cheese looks remarkably good.'

'Yes, it is,' said the old woman, putting it away. 'Very nice indeed. Nice bit of cheese.'

Mr Cercorelli sighed, and stood up.

'If you hear any more of this desperate rogue,' he said, 'be sure to let me know. Mr Buffaloni is offering a very generous reward. Good evening to you.'

CHAPTER FOUR

THE TRAVELLING PLAYERS

After a good night's sleep under a hedge, the Scarecrow and his servant woke up on a bright and sparkling morning.

'This is the life, Jack!' said the Scarecrow. 'The open road, the fresh air, and adventure just around the corner.'

'The fresh air's all right for you, master,' said Jack, removing leaves from his hair, 'but I like sleeping in a bed. I haven't seen a bed for so long, I can't remember whether the sheets go under the blankets or the blankets go under the sheets.'

'I shall just go and pay my respects to a colleague,' said the Scarecrow.

They'd woken up to find themselves close to a crossroads. A wooden sign stood where the roads met; but what the four arms were pointing to was impossible to read, for years of sun and rain had completely worn away the paint.

29

The Scarecrow strode up to the road sign and greeted it courteously. The sign took no notice, and neither did Jack, who was busy cutting a slice of cold meat with his little pocket knife, and folding it inside a slice of bread.

Then there came a loud *crack!*

Jack looked up to see the Scarecrow, very angry, clouting the nearest arm of the signpost as hard as he could.

'Take that, you insolent rogue!' he cried, and punched it again.

Unfortunately the first punch must have loosened something in the sign, because when he punched it for the second time, all four arms swung round, and the next one clonked the Scarecrow hard on the back of the head.

The Scarecrow fell over, shouting, 'Treachery! Cowardice!' and then bounced up at once, and seized the arm that had hit him and wrenched it off the signpost altogether.

'Take that, you dastardly footpad!' he cried, belabouring the post with the broken arm. 'Fight fairly, or surrender!'

The trouble was that every time he hit the post, it swung around again and hit him from the other side. However, he stood his ground, and fought back bravely.

'Master! Master!' called Jack, jumping up. 'That's not a footpad—that's a road sign!'

'He's in disguise,' said the Scarecrow. 'Mind out—stand back—he's a footpad all right. But don't you worry, I'll deal with him.'

'Right you are, master. Footpad he is, if you say so. But I think he's had enough now. I'm sure I heard him say, *I surrender.*'

'Did you? Are you sure?'

'Absolutely certain, master.'

'In that case—' began the Scarecrow, but stopped and looked down in horror at his own right arm, which was slipping slowly out of the sleeve of his jacket. The rake handle had come away from the broomstick that was his spine.

'I've been disarmed!' the Scarecrow said, shocked.

In fact, as Jack saw, the rake handle was so dry and brittle that it had never been much use in the first place, and the punishment it had taken in the fight with the road sign had cracked it in several places.

'I've got an idea, master,' he said. 'This fellow's arm is in better condition than your old one. Why don't we slip that up your sleeve instead?'

'What a good idea!' said the Scarecrow, cheering up at once.

So Jack did that, and just as had happened with the stick that had become his leg, the arm gave a kind of twitch when it met his shoulder, and settled into place at once.

'My word,' said the Scarecrow, admiring his new arm, trying it out by waving it around, and practising pointing at things with the finger on the end. 'What gifts you have, Jack, my boy! You could be a surgeon. Or a carpenter, even. And as for you, you scoundrel,' he added severely to the road sign, 'let that be a lesson to you.'

'I don't suppose he'll attack anyone else, master,' said Jack. 'I reckon you've sorted him out for good. Which way shall we go next?'

'That way,' said the Scarecrow, pointing confidently along one of the roads with his new arm.

So Jack shouldered his bag, and they set off.

After an hour's brisk walking, they reached the edge of a town. It must have been market day, because people were making for the town with carts full of vegetables and cheeses and other things to sell. One man was a bird-catcher. His cart was piled high with cages containing little songbirds such as linnets,  larks and goldfinches. The Scarecrow was very interested.

'Prisoners of war,' he explained to Jack. 'I expect they're being sent back to their own country.'

'I don't think so, master. I think people are going to buy them and keep them in cages so they can hear them singing.'

'No!' exclaimed the Scarecrow. 'No, no, people wouldn't do that. Why, that would be dishonourable. Take it from me, they're prisoners of war.'

Presently they came to the market place, and the Scarecrow gazed around in amazement at the town hall, the church, the market stalls.

'I had no idea civilization had advanced to this point,' he said to Jack. 'Why, this almost compares to Bella Fontana. What industry! What beauty! What splendour! You wouldn't find a place like this in the kingdom of the birds, I'm sure of that.'

Jack could see children whispering and pointing at the Scarecrow.

'Listen, master,' he said, 'I don't think we—'

'What's *that*?' said the Scarecrow, full of excitement.

He was pointing at a canvas booth where a carpenter was hammering some planks together to hold up a brightly painted picture of a wild landscape.

'That's going to be a play,' said Jack. 'That's called scenery. Actors come out in front of it and act out a story.'

The Scarecrow's eyes were open as wide as they could go. He moved towards the booth as if he were being pulled on a string. There was a big colourful poster nearby, and a man was reading it aloud for those people who couldn't read themselves:

'*The Tragical History of Harlequin and Queen Dido*,' the man read out. '*To be acted by Signor Rigatelli's Celebrated Players, late from triumphs in Paris, Venice, Madrid, and Constantinople. With Effects of Battle and Shipwreck, a Dance of the Infernal Spirits, and the Eruption of Vesuvius. Daily at noon, mid-afternoon, and sunset, with special evening performance complete with Pyrotechnical Extravaganza.*'

The Scarecrow was nearly floating with excitement.

'I want to watch it *all*!' he said. 'Again and again!'

'Well, it's not free, master,' Jack explained. 'You have to pay. And we haven't got any money.'

'In that case,' said the Scarecrow, 'I shall have to offer my services as an actor. I say!' he called. 'Signor Rigatelli!'

33

A fat man wearing a dressing gown and eating a piece of salami came out from behind the scenery.

'Yes?' he said.

'Signor Rigatelli,' began the Scarecrow, 'I—'

'Blimey,' said Signor Rigatelli to Jack, 'that's good. Do some more.'

'I'm not doing anything,' Jack said.

'Excuse me,' said the Scarecrow, 'but I—'

'That's it! Brilliant!' said Rigatelli.

'*What?*' said Jack. 'What are you talking about?'

'Ventriloquism,' said Rigatelli. 'Do it again, go on.'

'Signor Rigatelli,' said the Scarecrow once more, 'my patience is not inexhaustible. I have the honour to present myself to you as an actor of modest experience but boundless genius . . . What are you doing?'

Signor Rigatelli was walking around the Scarecrow, studying him from every angle. Then he lifted up the back of the Scarecrow's jacket to see how he worked, and the Scarecrow leaped away, furious.

'No—it's all right, master, don't get cross,' said Jack hastily. 'It's just that he'd like to be an actor, you see,' he explained to Rigatelli, 'and I'm his agent,' he added.

'I've never seen anything like it,' said the great showman. 'I can't see how it works at all. Tell you what, we'll use him as a prop in the mad scene. He can stand there on the blasted heath when the queen goes barmy. Then if he looks all right he can go on again as an infernal spirit. Can you make him dance?'

'I'm not sure,' said Jack.

'Well, he can follow the others. First call in ten

34

minutes.'

And Rigatelli crammed the rest of the salami in his mouth, and went back inside his caravan.

The Scarecrow was ecstatic.

'A prop!' he said. 'I'm going to be a *prop*! Do you realize, Jack, that this is the first step on the road to a glorious career? And already I'm playing a prop! He must have been very impressed.'

'Yes,' said Jack, 'probably.'

The Scarecrow was already disappearing behind the scenery.

'Master,' said Jack, 'wait . . .'

He found the Scarecrow watching with great interest as an actor, sitting in front of a mirror, put his greasepaint on.

'Good grief!' the actor said, suddenly catching sight of the Scarecrow, and leaped out of his chair, dropping his greasepaint.

'Good day, sir,' said the Scarecrow. 'Allow me to introduce myself. I am to play the part of a prop.

May I trouble you for the use of your make-up?'

The actor swallowed hard and looked around. Then he saw Jack.

'Who's this?' he said.

'This is Lord Scarecrow,' said Jack, 'and Signor Rigatelli says he can take part in the mad scene. Listen, master,' he said to the Scarecrow, who was sitting down and looking with great interest at all the pots of greasepaint and powder. 'You know what a prop is, don't you?'

'It's a very important part,' said the Scarecrow, painting a pair of bright red lips on the front of his turnip.

'Yes, but it's what they call a silent role,' said Jack. 'You don't move and you don't speak.'

'What's going on?' said the actor.

'*I'm* going on!' said the Scarecrow proudly. 'In the mad scene.'

He outlined each of his eyes with black, and then dabbed some red powder on his cheeks. The actor was watching, goggle-eyed.

'That looks lovely, master,' Jack said, 'but you don't want to overdo it.'

'You think we should be subtle?'

'For the mad scene, definitely, master.'

'Very well. Perhaps a wig would make me look more subtle.'

'Not that one,' said Jack, taking a big blond curly wig out of the Scarecrow's hands. 'Just remember—don't move and don't speak.'

'I'll do it all with my eyes,' said the Scarecrow, taking the wig back and settling it over his turnip.

The actor gave him a horrified look and left.

'I need a costume now,' said the Scarecrow. 'This'll do.'

He picked up a scarlet cloak and twirled it around his shoulders. Jack clutched his head in despair, and followed the Scarecrow out behind the scenes, where the actors and the musicians and the stage hands were getting everything ready. There was a lot to look at, and Jack had to stop the Scarecrow explaining it all to him.

'Yes, master—hush now—the audience is out there, so we all have to be quiet . . .'

'There it is!' said an angry actress, and snatched the wig off the Scarecrow's head. 'What are you playing at?' she said to Jack. 'How dare you put my wig on that thing?'

'I beg your pardon,' said the Scarecrow, getting to his feet and bowing very low. 'I would not upset you for the world, madam, but you are already so beautiful that you need no improvement; whereas I . . .'

The actress was watching with critical interest as she settled the wig on her head.

'Not bad,' she said to Jack. 'I've seen a lot worse. I can't see how you move him at all. But don't you touch my stuff again, you hear?'

'Sorry,' said Jack.

The actress swept away.

'Such grace! Such beauty!' said the Scarecrow, gazing after her.

'Yes, master, but *shush*!' said Jack. 'Sit *down*. Be *quiet.*'

Just then they heard a crash of cymbals and a blast on a trumpet.

'Ladies and gentlemen!' came the voice of Signor Rigatelli. 'We present a performance of the doleful and piteous tragedy of Harlequin and Queen Dido, with pictorial and scenic effects never before seen,

37

and featuring the most comical interludes ever presented on the public stage! Our performance today is sponsored by the Buffaloni Dried Meat Company, the makers of the finest salami in town, A Smile In Every Bite.'

The Buffalonis again, thought Jack. They get up to everything.

There was a roll of drums, and the curtain went up. Jack and the Scarecrow watched wide-eyed as the play began. It wasn't much of a story, but the audience enjoyed Harlequin pretending to lose a string of sausages, and then swallowing a fly by mistake and leaping around the stage as it buzzed inside him; and then Queen Dido was abandoned by her lover, Captain Fanfarone, and ran offstage mad with grief. She was the actress in the blond wig.

'Here! Boy!' came a loud whisper from Rigatelli. 'Get him on! It's the mad scene! Stick him in the middle and get off quick.'

The Scarecrow spread his arms wide as Jack carried him onstage.

'I shall be the best prop there ever was!' he declared. 'They'll be talking about my prop for years to come.'

Jack put his finger to his lips and tiptoed offstage. As he did, he found himself face to face with the actress playing Queen Dido, who was about to come on again. She looked furious.

'What's that thing doing?' she demanded.

'He's a prop,' Jack explained.

'If you make him move or speak I'll skin you alive,' she said. 'Manually.'

Jack swallowed and nodded hard.

The curtain rose, and Jack jumped, because

38

Queen Dido gave a wild, unearthly shriek and ran past him on to the stage.

'Oh! Ah! Woe! Misery!' she screamed, and flung herself to the ground.

The audience watched, enthralled. So did the Scarecrow. Jack could see his eyes getting wider and following her as she grovelled and shrieked and pretended to tear her hair.

'Hey nonny nonny,' she wailed, and danced up and down blowing kisses at the air. 'There's rosemary, that's for remembrance! Hey nonny nonny! O, Fanfarone, thou art a villain, forsooth! It was a lover and his lass! There's a daisy for you. La, la, la!'

Jack was very impressed. It certainly looked like great acting.

Suddenly she sat down and began to pluck the petals out of an imaginary daisy.

'He loves me—he loves me not—he loves me—he loves me not—oh, daisy, daisy, give me your answer, do! Oh, that my heart would boil over and put out the fires of my grief! La, la, la, Fanfarone, thou art a pretty villain!'

Jack was watching the Scarecrow closely. He could see the poor booby getting more and more worried, and he whispered, 'Don't, master—it's not real—keep still!'

The Scarecrow was trying, that was clear. He only moved his head very slowly to follow what Queen Dido was doing, but he did move it, and already one or two people in the audience had noticed and were nudging their neighbours to point him out.

Queen Dido struggled to her feet, clutching her heart. Suddenly the Scarecrow noticed that she had a dagger in her hand. She had her back to him, and she couldn't see him leaning sideways to peer round at her, a look of alarm on his great knobbly face.

'Oh! Ah! Woe! The pangs of my sorrow tear at my soul like red-hot hooks! Ahhhhhhhh . . .'

She gave a long despairing cry, beginning as high as she could squeal and descending to the lowest note she could reach. She was famous for that cry. Critics had said that it plumbed the depths of mortal anguish, that it would melt a heart of stone, that no-one could hear it without feeling the tears gush from their eyes.

This time, though, she had the feeling that the audience wasn't quite with her. Some of them were laughing, even, and what made it worse was that when she spun round to see if it was the Scarecrow they were laughing at, he instantly remembered to act, and fell still, staring out as if he was nothing but a turnip on a stick.

Queen Dido gave him a look of furious suspicion, and resolved to try her famous cry again.

'*Waaahhh—aahhh—aaaahhhh . . .*' she wailed, wobbling and quavering all the way from a bat-like squeak down to a groan like a cow with a belly-ache.

And behind her the Scarecrow found himself moving in time with her, and imitating the way she wobbled her head and waved her arms and sank gradually downwards. He couldn't help it—he was deeply moved. Of course, the audience thought it was hilarious, and they roared, they slapped their thighs, they clapped and whistled and cheered.

Queen Dido was furious. And so was Signor Rigatelli. He suddenly appeared beside Jack and shoved two actors out on to the stage, saying, 'Get him off! Get him off!'

Unfortunately, the two actors were dressed as brigands, and sure enough the Scarecrow thought they were real.

'You villains!' he cried, and leaped forward with his wooden arms held out like fists. 'Your Majesty, get behind me! I'll defend you!'

And he bounced around the stage, aiming blows at the actors. Queen Dido, meanwhile, had stamped in rage and hurled her wig to the ground before storming offstage to shout at Rigatelli.

The audience was loving it.

'Go it, Scarecrow!' they shouted, and 'Whack 'em, Turnip! Look behind you! Up the Scarecrow!'

The two actors didn't know what to make of it, but they kept on chasing the Scarecrow and then having to run away when he fought back.

Suddenly the Scarecrow stopped, and pointed in horror at the blond wig on the boards in front of him.

'You cut her head off when I wasn't looking!' he cried. 'How dare you! Right, that does it. I'm really angry now!'

And waving his wooden arms like a windmill, he leaped at the two actors and belaboured them mercilessly. The audience went wild. But the actors were getting cross now, and they fought back, and then Rigatelli himself came bustling up to try and restore order.

Jack rushed onstage as well, to try and pull the Scarecrow away before he got hurt. Unfortunately one of the actors had got hold of the Scarecrow's left arm, and was tugging and tugging at it, while the Scarecrow was whacking him around the head; and when Jack seized the Scarecrow around the middle and tried to tug him backwards, his master's left arm came away entirely, and the actor holding it fell back suddenly into Rigatelli, knocking him back into the other actor, who grabbed at the scenery to save himself; but the combined weight of the three of them was too much for the blasted heath, and it all came down with a screech of wood and a tearing of canvas, and in a moment there was nothing to be seen but a heap of painted scenery heaving and cursing, with arms and legs waving and disappearing and emerging again.

'This way, master!' Jack said, hauling the Scarecrow off the stage. 'Let's run for it!'

'Never!' cried the Scarecrow. 'I shall never surrender!'

'It's not surrendering, master, it's beating a retreat,' said Jack, dragging him away.

Everyone in the market place had heard what was going on, and they'd left their stalls to go and laugh at the actors and the collapsing theatre. Among them was the bird-catcher. All his cages with their linnets and goldfinches were glittering in the sun, and the little birds were singing as loud as they could, and the Scarecrow couldn't resist.

'Birds,' he said very sternly, 'I accept that a state of war exists between your kingdom and me, but there is such a thing as justice. To see you imprisoned in this cruel way makes the blood rush to my turnip with indignation.

I am going to set you free, and I charge you on your honour to go straight home and not eat any farmer's grain on the way.'

Jack didn't notice what his master was doing, because he'd spotted an old man sitting at a stall selling umbrellas. He was too rheumaticky to run over to the theatre with everybody else, and he was pleased to sell one of his umbrellas to Jack, who had found a gold coin in a corner of the brigands' bag.

Then someone shouted, 'Stop thief! Get away from my birds!'

44

Jack turned round to see the Scarecrow opening the last of the cages. A flock of little birds was wheeling around his head, chirping merrily, and he was waving his one arm, the one that pointed nowhere.

'Fly!' he shouted. 'Fly away!'

'Come on, master!' called Jack. 'They're all after us now!' And he dragged the Scarecrow away, and the two of them fled as fast as they could. The cries of anger, the shouts of laughter, the full-throated singing of the liberated birds all gradually faded behind them.

When they reached the open country again, they stopped. Jack was out of breath. The Scarecrow was looking at himself, trying to work out what was wrong, and then he cried, 'Oh no! My other arm's gone! I'm falling to pieces!'

'Don't worry, master, I've thought of that. I bought you a new arm—look,' said Jack, and he slipped the umbrella up the Scarecrow's sleeve, handle first.

'Good gracious,' said the Scarecrow. 'I do believe—I think I—yes, yes, I can! Look at this! Just look at this, Jack!'

And he shook his new arm, and the umbrella opened. His great turnip-face, with its bright red mouth and black-rimmed eyes, was radiant.

'Aren't I clever!' he said, marvelling. 'Look at the ingenuity of it! It goes up—it comes down—it goes up—it comes down—'

'You can keep the sun off us, master,' said Jack. 'And the rain.'

The Scarecrow looked at him proudly. 'You'll go a long way, my boy!' he said. 'I was going to think of those things in a minute, but you beat me to it.

And what a triumph we had on the stage! We saw everything they said on the poster.'

'We didn't have the Shipwreck, though, or the Eruption of Vesuvius.'

'Oh, we will, Jack,' said the Scarecrow confidently. 'I'm sure we will.'

CHAPTER FIVE

SCARECROW FOR HIRE

When the lawyer reached the town next morning, he found it full of strange rumours. After interviewing Mr Rigatelli and the actress who played Queen Dido, who were both convinced that the Scarecrow was an automaton controlled by mesmeric waves as part of a plot organized by a rival theatre company, Mr Cercorelli found his way to the elderly umbrella salesman.

'Yes, I seen it all,' said the old man. 'It was a boy with a horan-gatang. I seen one of 'em before. They live in the trees in Borneo. Almost human they are, but you wouldn't mistake him close up. What d'you want him for? Has he escaped from a zoo?'

'Not exactly,' said Mr Cercorelli. 'Which way did they go?'

'That way,' said the old man, pointing. 'You'll recognize 'em easy enough. They bought one of my umbrellas.'

*   *   *

The Scarecrow and his servant walked a long way that day. They spent the night under a hedge by an olive grove, and the moment they woke up, Jack knew something was wrong.

He sat up and looked all around. The sun was shining, the air smelled of thyme and sage, there was the sound of little bells around the necks of a herd of goats browsing nearby; but something was missing.

'Master! Wake up! Our bag's been stolen!' Jack cried in despair, as soon as he realized what had happened. 'All the food's gone!'

The Scarecrow sat up at once, and opened his umbrella in alarm. Jack was lifting stones, peering under the hedge, running backwards and forwards to look up and down the road.

The Scarecrow peered into the ditch, frowning at a lizard. It took no notice. Then he bent over and looked at something among the leaves.

'A clue!' he called, and Jack came running.

'What, master?'

'There,' said the Scarecrow, using his pointing hand to indicate something small and unpleasant at his feet.

'What is it?'

'An owl pellet. You can take it from me, this was left by the culprit. No doubt about it, the thief is an owl.'

'Oh,' said Jack, scratching his head.

'Or a jackdaw,' the Scarecrow went on. 'In fact, now I think of it, it must have been a jackdaw, and he left the owl pellet to throw us off the scent. Can you believe the villainy of these birds! They have no shame.'

'No,' said Jack. 'None at all. Anyway, we haven't got any money, and we haven't got any food. I don't know what we're going to do.'

'We shall have to work for our living, dear boy,' said the Scarecrow cheerfully. 'But we are full of enterprise and both in the pink of health. Ow! Ow! What are you doing?'

His last words were spoken to a goat, which had come up behind him and started to make a meal of his trousers.

The Scarecrow turned and clouted the goat with his road sign. But the goat objected to this, and butted him hard, knocking him over before Jack could catch him. The Scarecrow was astonished.

'How dare you! What a cowardly attack!' he said, struggling up.

The goat charged him again. This time the Scarecrow was prepared. He opened his umbrella suddenly, and the goat skidded to a halt and started to eat that instead.

'Oh, really,' said the Scarecrow, 'this is too much!'

And then a tug-of-war began, with the goat at one end and the Scarecrow at the other. The rest of the goats came over to see what was happening, and one of them started nibbling at the Scarecrow's coat tails, another at his trousers, and a third began to browse on the straw coming out of his chest.

'Go on! Scram! Clear off!' Jack shouted, clapping his hands, and reluctantly the goats slouched away.

'You expect that sort of behaviour from people with feathers,' the Scarecrow said severely, 'not people with horns. I'm very disappointed.'

'They were taking a consuming interest in you, master,' said Jack.

'Well, you can't blame them for that,' said the Scarecrow, brushing his lapels and shaking out the remains of his coat. 'But I must say, Jack, they shouldn't be allowed out without a goatherd. We shan't let that happen in Spring Valley.'

'Spring Valley? Oh, I remember. How did you manage to get a big estate, all full of—what was it?—a farm and streams and wells and so on?'

'Well, it's a puzzle, Jack,' the Scarecrow admitted, as they set off along the road. 'I've always had an inner conviction that I was a man of property. A sort of gentleman farmer, you know.'

'And is that where we're going, Spring Valley?'

'In good time, Jack. We have to make our fortunes first.'

'Oh, I see. Well, look,' said Jack, pointing ahead of them, 'there's a farm, and a farmer. Let's go and ask him for a job. That'll be a start.'

The farmer was sitting disconsolately outside his house, sharpening a scythe.

'You want a job?' he said to Jack. 'You couldn't have come at a better . . . you know. The soldiers took all my, umm, away, and the birds are eating the, er, as fast as it comes up. You set up your, that, him, in the top field, and you can take the rattle and work in the orchard.'

'The thing is,' said Jack, 'he's getting a bit tattered. If you had a spare pair of trousers he'd look a lot more realistic.'

'There's a dirty old pair of, umm, you know, in the woodshed. Help yourself. There'll be a bite to, er, at sunset, and you can sleep in the barn.'

Soon afterwards, they were at work. The Scarecrow shooed away all the birds from the cornfield, and from time to time he opened and shut his umbrella, just to teach them a lesson. Jack roamed up and down the orchard, rattling hard whenever he saw a finch or a linnet.

It was hard work. The sun was hot and there were plenty of birds to scare. Jack found himself thinking about Spring Valley, and the Scarecrow's great estate. The poor noodle must have made it up and found himself believing it, Jack thought. He was good at that. It sounded like a nice place, though.

At sunset Jack stopped rattling, and went to call the Scarecrow in. His master was very impressed by the rattle.

51

'Formidable!' he said when Jack showed him how it worked. 'What a weapon! I don't suppose I could use it tomorrow?'

'Well, if you do, master, I won't have anything to scare the birds with. You're an expert, and you can do it just by looking at them, but I need all the help I can get. Now you go and sit down in the barn, and I'll fetch us some supper.'

The farmer's wife gave Jack a pot of stew and a big hunk of bread, and told him not to come in the kitchen with that monster of his. New-fangled bird-scarers were all very well, but this was a respectable farm, and she couldn't be doing with mechanical monsters in the house.

'Righto, missus,' said Jack. 'Any chance of a drink?'

'There's a bucket in the well,' she said, 'and a tin cup on a string next to it.'

'Thank you,' said Jack, and took his pot of stew to the barn, pausing for a good long swig of water on the way.

But before he went into the barn, he stopped outside, because he could hear voices.

'Oh, yes,' the Scarecrow was saying, 'we fought off a dozen brigands, my servant and I.'

'Brigands?' said someone else. It was a female voice, and it was full of admiration.

Jack walked in to find the Scarecrow sitting on a bale of straw, surrounded by a dozen rakes and hoes and broomsticks and spades and pitchforks. They were all leaning on the wall, listening respectfully.

At least, that's what it looked like until they realized Jack was there. Then they went back to looking like rakes and hoes and so on.

52

'Ah, Jack, my boy!' said the Scarecrow.

'The farmer's wife gave me a bowl of stew for us,' said Jack doubtfully, looking around.

'You have most of it,' said the Scarecrow. 'I don't eat a great deal. A small piece of bread will be quite sufficient.'

So Jack sat down and tucked into the stew, which was full of peppers and onions and bits of gristly sausage.

'I thought I heard voices, master,' he said with his mouth full.

'And so you did. I was just telling these ladies and gentlemen about our adventures.'

Jack looked around at the rakes and hoes and brooms. None of them moved or said a word.

'Ah,' said Jack. 'Right.'

'As I was saying,' the Scarecrow went on, 'the brigands were a fearsome crew. Armed to the teeth, every single one. They trapped us in their cave and—'

'I thought you said it was a ruined castle,' said a rake.

'That's right, a ruined castle,' said the Scarecrow

53

cheerfully.

Jack's hair was standing on end. It certainly seemed as if one of the rakes had spoken, but it was getting dark, and he was very tired. He rubbed his eyes, and felt them closing as fast as he could rub them open again.

'Well, which?' demanded the rake.

'Castle. Next to a cave. My servant and I went in to investigate, and the next thing we knew, in came two dozen brigands. Or three dozen, probably. I hid in the corner, and Jack told them a story to send them to sleep, and then I loomed up like an apparition—like this—'

The Scarecrow raised his arms and made a hideous face. Some of the smaller brooms flinched away, and a little fork squeaked in terror.

'And the brigands turned tail and fled,' the Scarecrow went on. 'I've thought about it since, and I've worked out the reason why. I think they were birds, and they were only disguised as brigands. Big birds,' he explained. 'Sort of ostrich-sized. Very dangerous,' he added.

'You must be very brave,' said a broom shyly.

'Oh, I don't know,' said the Scarecrow. 'One gets used to danger in this line of work. But soon after that, I entered a new profession. I went on the stage!'

Jack was lying down now. The last thing he noticed before he fell asleep was the Scarecrow beginning to act out the role he had taken in the play; only it seemed a much more important role than Jack remembered, and when it got to the point where Queen Dido fell in love with the Scarecrow and made him Prime Minister, Jack realized he'd been asleep for some time.

He woke up to find the sun in his eyes and the Scarecrow shaking him.

'Jack! Wake up! Time for work! The birds have been up for some time. But Jack—I need to have a word with you. In private.'

Jack rubbed his eyes and looked around.

'We *are* in private,' he said.

'No! I mean *more* private,' the Scarecrow said, in an urgent whisper. 'Away from—you know . . .'

He gestured over his shoulder and nodded backwards in a meaningful way.

'Ah, I see,' said Jack, who had no idea what he was talking about. 'Just give me a moment, and I'll meet you out by the well, master.'

The Scarecrow nodded and strode out of the barn. Jack scratched his head. The rakes and hoes and brooms were perfectly still and silent.

'Must have been dreaming,' Jack said to himself, and got up.

The farmer's wife gave him some bread and jam for breakfast, and Jack took it out to the well, where the Scarecrow was waiting impatiently.

'What is it, master?' he said.

'I've decided to get married,' the Scarecrow told him. 'As a matter of fact I've fallen in love. Oh, Jack, she's so beautiful! And such a delicate nature! You'd never believe it, but I feel almost clumsy beside her. Her grace! Her charm! Oh, my heart is lost, I love her, I worship the ground she brushes!'

'Brushes?' said Jack, his mouth full.

'She's a broom,' the Scarecrow explained. 'You must have noticed her. The very pretty one! The lovely one! Oh, I adore her!'

'Have you told her?'

56

'Ah. That's what I was going to tell you. I haven't got the nerve, Jack. My courage fails me. As soon as I look at her I feel like a—like a—like an onion.'

'An onion?'

'Yes, just like an onion. But I can't think of a thing to say. So *you'll* have to tell her.'

Jack scratched his head.

'Well,' he said, 'I'm not as eloquent as you are, master. I'd probably get it all wrong. I'm sure she'd rather hear it from you.'

'Well, of course she would,' agreed the Scarecrow. 'Anyone would. But I'm struck dumb when I see her, so it'll have to be you.'

'I don't understand why you feel like an onion,' Jack said.

'No, neither do I. I had no idea that love would have that effect. Have you ever been in love, Jack?'

'I don't think so. If I fell in love, I'd probably feel like a turnip. Listen, I tell you what, master—'

'I know! You could pretend to be a bird, and attack her, and I could pretend to come and fight you off. I bet she'd be impressed by that.'

'I'm not a good actor like you, master. She'd probably guess I wasn't a real bird. Listen, let's go and do some work, and you can think about her all day long, out in the cornfield. We'll talk about it later, before we come in.'

'Yes! That's a good idea,' said the Scarecrow, and marched off proudly to start the day's work.

CHAPTER SIX

A SERENADE

Jack worked hard all morning. At midday the farmer came into the orchard to see how he was getting on, and looked around approvingly.

'That other fellow,' he said, 'your mate . . .'

'My master,' said Jack.

'As you like. Him. He's a good worker, and no mistake. But . . . well . . . you know.'

'Oh, he's good at scarecrowing,' said Jack.

'No doubt about it. But—umm—he's a bit, er, well, isn't he?'

'Only if you don't know him.'

'Oh, is that right? Then he's . . . mmm . . . is he?'

'He's a deep character,' said Jack, rattling at a blackbird.

'Ah,' said the farmer. 'Thing is, he looks almost— well, if I didn't know better, I'd even say . . . you know.'

'That's part of his cleverness. See, when he's working, he never . . . kind of thing.'

'No,' said the farmer. 'Wouldn't do to . . . umm.'

'I mean, there'd be no end of a—you know.'

'Too true. You're right there. All the same, eh? I mean . . .'

'Yes,' agreed Jack. 'No. It'd be terrible if . . . er.'

'A word to the wise, eh?' said the farmer, and winked and tapped the side of his nose. Jack did the same, in case it was the private signal of a secret society. The farmer nodded and went away.

Well, it's a good thing he didn't go and say all that to the master, Jack thought. The poor booby wouldn't have understood a word.

He rattled away busily all afternoon, and as the sun was setting he went to call the Scarecrow from the top field.

'Jack,' said the Scarecrow, 'I've been thinking about her all day long, just as you suggested, and I've come to the conclusion that if she won't marry me, I'll have to do something desperate.'

'Oh dear,' said Jack. 'What would that be, master?'

'I'm saving that till tomorrow to think about.'

'Good idea. I wonder what's for supper?'

The farmer's wife gave them another bowl of stew, and she gave the Scarecrow a long hard suspicious look, too, which he didn't see, because he was gazing at the barn with a dopey expression on his turnip.

'Thank you, missus,' Jack said.

'You mind you keep him locked up at night,' said the farmer's wife. 'I don't like the look of him. If I find any hens missing . . .'

Jack and his master sat down beside the well, and once again the Scarecrow let Jack have all the stew, and only nibbled at a piece of bread.

59

'You ought to eat something, master,' said Jack. 'I bet she'd like you just as much if you had a full belly. You'd feel better, anyway.'

'No, I've got no appetite, Jack. I'm wasting away with love.'

'If you're sure, then,' said Jack, finishing off the stew.

'I know!' said the Scarecrow, sitting up suddenly and opening his umbrella with excitement. 'I could serenade her!'

'Well—' said Jack, but the Scarecrow was too excited to listen.

'Yes! That's it! Here's the plan. Wait till dark, and then pick her up and pretend to sweep the floor. And sweep her outside, and then sort of casually lean her against the wall, and then I'll sing to her.'

'Well—' Jack began again.

'Oh, yes. When she hears me sing, her heart will be mine!'

'You better not sing too loud. I don't think the farmer'd like it. I'm sure his old lady wouldn't.'

'Oh, I shall be very discreet,' said the Scarecrow. 'Tender, but ardent, is the note to strike.'

'That sounds about right,' said Jack.

'Start sweeping as soon as the moon shines into the farmyard. I think moonlight would show me to advantage, don't you?'

'Maybe you better let me tidy you up,' said Jack, and he dusted the Scarecrow's shoulders, and put some fresh straw in his chest, and washed his turnip. 'There—you look a treat. Remember—not too loud, now.'

The Scarecrow sat down outside the barn, and Jack went inside to lie down. Before he did, though, he found the broom and put her beside the door, so that he'd be able to find her in the dark.

'Excuse me,' he found himself saying, 'but I hope you don't mind if I put you over here. You'll find out why when the moon comes up.'

She didn't reply, but she leaned against the wall very gracefully. Jack thought she must be shy, until he caught himself and shook his head.

He's got me believing she's alive, he thought. I better be careful, in case I go as mad as he is.

He lay down on the straw and closed his eyes. The old donkey and the cow were asleep on their feet, just breathing quietly and chewing a bit from time to time, and it was all very quiet and peaceful.

Jack woke up when the moonlight touched his eyes. He yawned and stretched and sat up.

'Well,' he said to himself, 'time to start brushing the floor. This is a daft idea. Still, he's a marvel, the master, no doubt about it.'

He took the broom and swept the floor, brushing all the straw and dust casually towards the door where the moonlight was shining through. Once he was outside, he leaned the broom against the wall and yawned again before going back to lie down.

And almost at once he went back to sleep. He must have started dreaming straight away, because it seemed as if he were watching the Scarecrow

61

sweeping the ground outside, singing to the broom as he did so:

> 'Your handle so slender,
> Your bristles so tender,
> I have to surrender
>   My heart to your charms;
> Retreating, advancing,
> And secretly glancing,
> Oh, never stop dancing
>   All night in my arms!'

Jack blinked and rubbed his eyes, but it made no difference. The Scarecrow and the broom were waltzing around the barnyard like the most graceful dancers at a ball.

> 'Your gentle demeanour
> Sweeps everything cleaner!
> I never have seen a
>   More elegant Miss;
> So gracious, so charming,
> Completely disarming,
> Oh where is the harm in
>   A maidenly kiss?'

Jack thought, He's going to marry her, and then he won't want a servant any more. Mind you, he does look happy. But I don't know if I'll ever find a master I'd rather serve . . .

And while he was lying there puzzled by all those thoughts, he was woken up all of a sudden by a horrible raucous yell.

'*Hee-haw! Hee-haw!*'

He sat up, and realized first that it *had* been a dream; and second, that the old donkey in the barn was braying and stamping and creating no end of a fuss; and third, that outside in the barnyard the Scarecrow was roaring and howling and bellowing with anger, or distress, or misery.

Jack scrambled to the door of the barn to see the farmer's wife, in a long nightdress, running out of the kitchen door with a frying pan held high above her head. Behind her, the farmer, in a long nightshirt, was fumbling with a blunderbuss. The Scarecrow was clutching the broom to his heart, and real tears were streaming down his turnip.

'No, missus! No! Don't!' Jack shouted, and ran out to try and hold off the farmer's wife, who was about to wallop the Scarecrow with the frying pan. There was no danger from the farmer; as soon as he tried to aim the blunderbuss, all the lead shot fell out of the end of the barrel, and bounced on the flagstones like hail.

Jack reached the Scarecrow just as the farmer's wife did, and stood between them with his arms held wide.

'No, missus! Stop! Let me explain!' he said.

'I'll brain him!' she cried. 'I'll teach him to go caterwauling in the middle of the night and terrifying honest folk out of their beds!'

'No, don't, missus, he's a poor zany, he doesn't mean any harm—you leave him to me—'

'I told you!' said the farmer, staying safely behind his wife. 'Didn't I? Eh?'

'Yes, you did,' Jack agreed. 'You told me something, anyway.'

'None of this . . . you know,' the farmer added.

'You take that horrible thing away,' said the farmer's wife, 'and you get out of here right now, and don't you come back!'

'Certainly, missus,' said Jack, 'and what about our wages?'

'Wages?' she said. 'You're not getting any wages. Clear off, you and your monster both!'

Jack turned to the Scarecrow, who hadn't heard any of what the farmer's wife had said. In fact, he was still sobbing in despair.

'Now then, master, what's the trouble?' he said.

'She's already engaged!' the Scarecrow howled. 'She's going to marry a rake!'

'Oh, that's bad luck,' said Jack. 'Still, look on the bright side—'

'I shall do the decent thing, of course,' the Scarecrow went on, struggling to control his emotions. 'My dear young lady,' he said to the broom, 'nothing would make me stand between you and your happiness, if your heart is already given to the gentleman in the barn. But I warn him,' he said, raising his voice and looking in at all the tools leaning on the wall, 'he had better treat this broom like the precious creature she is, and make her happiness the centre of his life, or he will face my wrath!'

With a last choking sob, he handed the broom gently to Jack. Jack took her into the barn and stood her next to the rake.

When he got back outside, the Scarecrow was speaking to the farmer and his wife.

'I am sorry for waking you up,' he said, 'but I make no excuses for the passionate expression of my feelings. After all, that is the one thing that distinguishes us from the animals.'

'Mad,' said the farmer's wife. 'Barmy. Go on, get out, clear off down the road and don't come back.'

The Scarecrow bowed as gracefully as he could.

'Well, dear,' the farmer said, 'mustn't . . . you know. Not so many, umm, about these days, eh? Sort of thing . . .'

'He's raving mad, and I want him gone!' she said. 'Also he's a horrible-looking monster, and he's frightened the donkey. Scram!' she said again, raising the frying pan.

'Come on, master,' said Jack. 'We'll seek our fortune somewhere else. We've slept under hedges before, and it's a nice warm night.'

So side by side the Scarecrow and his servant set off down the moonlit road. From time to time the Scarecrow would sigh heavily and turn to look back with such a look of anguish on his turnip that Jack felt sure the broom would leave her rake and fall in love with him, if she could; but it was too late.

*　　　*　　　*

'Oh, yes,' said the farmer, 'he was definitely . . . you know.'

'Mad as a hatter!' said his wife. 'A dangerous lunatic. Foreign, too. Shouldn't have been let out.'

'I see,' said Mr Cercorelli. 'And when did he leave?'

'When was it now?' said the farmer. 'About . . . er . . .'

'Middle of the night,' snapped his wife. 'What d'you want to know for, anyway? You his keeper?'

'In a manner of speaking, that is so. I am charged by my employer to bring this scarecrow back where he belongs.'

'Ah,' said the farmer. 'So it's a case of, umm, is it?'

'I beg your pardon?'

'You know, touch of the old, er, as it were. Eh?'

Mr Cercorelli gathered his papers and stood up.

'You put it very accurately, sir,' he said. 'Thank you for your help.'

'You going to lock him up when you catch him?' demanded the farmer's wife.

'Oh, I can assure you,' said Mr Cercorelli, 'that is the least of it.'

CHAPTER SEVEN

THE MISTY CART

'Jack,' said the Scarecrow next morning, 'now that my heart is broken, I think we should set out on the open road and seek our fortune.'

'What about your estate in Spring Valley, master?'

'Ah, yes, indeed. We must earn enough money to set the place in order. Then we shall go back and look after it.'

I hope there's plenty of food there, Jack thought.

The Scarecrow strode out briskly, and Jack trotted along beside him. There were plenty of things to look at, and although the Scarecrow's heart was broken, his curiosity about the world was undimmed.

'Why has that building burned down?' he'd say, or 'I wonder why that old lady is climbing a ladder,' or 'D'you know, Jack, it's an extraordinary thing, but we haven't heard a bird for hours. Why would that be, do you think?'

'I think the soldiers have been here,' Jack told him. 'They probably burned the house down, and took all the farm workers away so the old lady's got to mend the roof herself. As for the birds—why, the soldiers must have eaten up all the food and left none for the birds, not even a grain of wheat.'

'Hmm,' said the Scarecrow. 'Soldiers, eh? Do they do that sort of thing?'

'They're the worst people in the world, soldiers,' said Jack.

'Worse than birds?'

'Much worse. The only thing to do when the soldiers come is hide, and keep very very quiet.'

'What do they look like?'

'Well—'

But before Jack could answer, the Scarecrow's attention was caught by something else.

'Look!' he cried, pointing in excitement. 'What's that?'

There was a caravan coming towards them, pulled by an ancient horse that was so skinny you could count all its ribs. The caravan was covered in painted stars and moons and mystic symbols, and sitting on the box holding the reins was a man almost as skinny as the horse, wearing a long pointed hat and a robe covered in more stars and moons.

The Scarecrow gazed at it all with great admiration.

As soon as he saw them, the man waved and shook the reins to make the horse stand still. The poor old beast was only too glad to have a rest. The man jumped off the box and scampered over to the Scarecrow.

'Good day to you, sir! Good day, my lord!' he

said, bowing low and plucking at the Scarecrow's
sleeve.

'Good day to *you*, sir,' the Scarecrow said.

'Master,' said Jack, 'I don't think—'

But the stranger with the mystic robes had seized
the Scarecrow's road-sign hand, and was
scrutinizing it closely.

'Ah!' he said. 'Aha! Ha! I see great fortune in this
hand!'

'Really?' said the Scarecrow, impressed. 'How do
you do that?'

'By means of the mystic arts!'

'Oh!' said the Scarecrow. 'Jack, we must get a
misty cart! Just like this gentleman's one. Then
we'd know things too. We could make our fortune
and find our way to Spring Valley and take it—'

'Spring Valley, did you say, sir?' said the stranger.
'Would you be a member of the celebrated
Buffaloni family, my lord?'

'I don't think so,' said the Scarecrow.

'Ah! I understand! They've called you in as a
consultant, to take it in hand. I hear that the
Buffalonis are doing splendid things in the field of
industry. Draining all those springs and wells and
putting up wonderful factories! Yes? No?'

Seeing that the Scarecrow was baffled, the
astrologer smoothly went on:

'But let me read your horoscope and look deep
into the crystal ball. Before the power of my gaze,
the veil of time is drawn aside and the mysteries of
the future are revealed. Come into my caravan for
a consultation!'

'Master,' Jack whispered, 'this'll cost us money,
and we haven't got any. Besides, he's an old
fraud—'

'Oh, no, my boy, you've got it wrong,' said the Scarecrow. 'I'm a pretty good judge, and this gentleman's mind is on higher things than fraud. His thoughts dwell in the realm of the sublime, Jack!'

'Quite right, sir! You are a profound and perceptive thinker!' said the mystic, beckoning them into the caravan, and uncovering a crystal ball on a little table.

They all sat down. Waving his fingers in a mystical way, the astrologer peered deeply into the crystal.

'Ah!' he said. 'As I suspected. The planetary fluminations are dark and obscure. The only way of disclarifying the astroplasm is to cast your horoscope, my dear sir, which I can do for a very modest fee.'

'Well, that's that then,' said Jack, standing up, 'because we haven't got a penny between us. Good day—'

'No, Jack, wait!' said the Scarecrow, banging his head.

'What are you doing, master?' said Jack. 'Stop it—you'll hurt yourself!'

'Ah—there it is!' cried the Scarecrow, and out of a crack in his turnip there fell a little gold coin.

Jack and the mystic pounced at once, but the mystic got there first.

'Excellent!' he said, nipping the coin between his long horse-like teeth. 'By a remarkable coincidence, this is exactly the right fee. I shall consult the stars at once.'

'Where did that gold coin come from, master?' said Jack, amazed.

'Oh, it's been in there for a while,' the Scarecrow told him.

'But—but—if—if—' Jack said, tearing his hair.

The Scarecrow took no notice. He was watching the astrologer, who took a dusty book from a shelf and opened it to show charts and columns of numbers, and ran a finger swiftly down them, muttering learnedly.

'You see what he's doing?' whispered the Scarecrow. 'This is clever, Jack, this is very deep.'

'Ahhhhh!' said the astrologer, in a long quavering wail. 'I see great fortune in the stars!'

'Go on, go on!' said the Scarecrow.

'Oh, yes,' said the mystic, licking a dirty finger and turning over several pages. 'And there is more!'

'You see, Jack? What a good thing we met this gentleman!' said the Scarecrow.

The astrologer suddenly drew in his breath, peering at the symbols in his book. So did the Scarecrow. They both held it for a long time, until the astrologer let it out in a long whistle. So did the Scarecrow.

Then, as if it was too heavy a burden to bear, the astrologer slowly lifted his head.

The Scarecrow's little muddy eyes were as wide as they could get—his straw was standing on end—his great gaping mouth hung open.

'I have never seen a destiny as strange and profound as this,' said the astrologer in a low, quavery voice. 'The paranomical ecliptic of the clavicle of Solomon, multiplied by the solar influence in the trine of the zaphoristical catanastomoid, divided by the meridian of the vernal azimuth and composticated by the diaphragm of Ezekiel, reveals . . .'

'Yes?'

'Means . . .'

'Yes? Yes?'

'Foretells . . .'

'Yes? Yes? Yes?'

The mystic paused for a moment, and his eyes swivelled to look at Jack, and then swivelled back to the Scarecrow.

'Danger,' he said solemnly.

'Oh no!' said the Scarecrow.

'Followed by joy—'

'Yes!'

'And then trouble—'

'No!'

'Leading to glory—'

'Yes!'

'Turning to sorrow—'

'No, no, no!'

73

The Scarecrow was in mortal fear.

The astrologer slowly closed the book and moved it out of Jack's reach. Then his upper lip drew back so suddenly that it made Jack jump. Beaming like a crocodile in Holy Orders, the old man said:

'But the suffering will be crowned with success—'

'Hoorah!' cried the Scarecrow.

'And the tears will end in triumph—'

'Thank goodness for that!'

'And health, wealth and happiness will be yours for as long as you live!'

'Oh, I'm so glad! Oh, what a relief!' said the Scarecrow. 'There you are, Jack, you see, this gentleman knows what he's talking about, all right. Oh, I was worried there! But it all came right in the end. Thank you, sir! A thousand thanks! We can go on our way with confidence and fortitude. My goodness, what an experience.'

'My pleasure,' said the mystic, bowing low. 'Take care as you leave. The steps are rickety. Good day!'

He gave Jack a suspicious look, and Jack gave him one in return.

'Just think of that, Jack,' said the Scarecrow in an awed and humble voice as the caravan slowly drew away. 'We have been inside a misty cart, and we have heard the secrets of the future!'

'Never mind that, master,' said Jack. 'Have you got any more money in your head?'

'Let me see,' said the Scarecrow, and he banged his turnip vigorously. Then he shook it hard. 'Hmm,' he said, 'something's rattling. Let me see . . .'

He turned his head sideways and shook it. Something fell out and bounced on the road.

The two of them bent over to look at it.

'It's a pea,' said Jack.

'Ah, yes,' said the Scarecrow modestly. 'That's my brain, you know.'

But before either of them could pick it up and put it back, a blackbird flew down, seized the pea in his beak, and flew up and perched on a branch.

The Scarecrow was outraged. He waved his road sign, he opened and shut his umbrella, and he stamped with fury.

'You scoundrel! You thief!' he roared. 'Give me my brain back!'

The blackbird swallowed the pea, and then, to Jack's astonishment, said, 'Get lost. I saw it first.'

'How dare you!' the Scarecrow shouted in reply. 'I've never known such unprincipled behaviour!'

'Don't shout at me,' whined the blackbird. 'You're cruel, you are. You got a horrible cruel face. I'll have the law on you if you shout at me. It's not fair.'

In fury, the Scarecrow opened and shut his umbrella several times, but in his rage he couldn't find any words, so the things he said sounded like this:

'R r r o w l — n n h n r r r — e e e e — m n m n m — n g n n m m g g r r n n n g g g — b b r r r — f f f f — s s s s — gggrrrssschhttt!'

The blackbird cringed, and uttering a feeble squeak, he flew away.

Jack scratched his head.

'I knew parrots could talk, master, but not blackbirds,' he said.

'Oh, they all can, Jack. You should hear the insolent way they speak to me when they think nobody else can hear. I expect that young scoundrel thought you were a scarecrow too, and he could get away with it.'

'Well, I'm learning new things all the time,' said Jack. 'Anyway, it seems to me, master, that until we find you a new brain, you'll have to try and get on without one. We managed to find you some new arms all right, remember.'

The Scarecrow had been stamping up and down, still furious, but he stopped and looked at Jack when he heard that, and calmed down at once.

'Do you think we could find another one?' he said.

'Can't be too hard,' said Jack. 'See how you get on without it at first. You might not need one at all. Like an appendix.'

'It's very personal, though,' said the Scarecrow doubtfully.

'We'll find something, don't worry.'

'Ah, Jack, my boy, employing you was the best decision I ever made! I can do without a brain, but I don't think I could do without my servant.'

'Well, thank you, master. But I don't think I can do without food. I hope we find something to eat soon.'

Since there was nothing to eat there, they set off along the road again. But it was a bleak and deserted sort of district; the only farms they passed were burned down, and there wasn't a single person in sight.

'No birds,' said the Scarecrow, looking around. 'It's a curious thing, Jack, but I don't like it when there aren't any birds.'

'I don't like it when there isn't any food,' said Jack.

'Look!' said the Scarecrow, pointing back along the road. 'What's that?'

All they could see was a cloud of dust. But there was a sound as well, and Jack recognized it at once: a regular tramp-tramp-tramp and the beats of a snare drum accompanying it. It was a regiment of soldiers.

Chapter Eight

The Pride of the Regiment

Jack tugged at the Scarecrow's sleeve.
'Come on, master!' he said urgently. 'We'll hide till they've gone past!'
The Scarecrow followed Jack into a clump of bushes.

'Are we allowed to look at them?' he said.

'Yes, but don't let them see us, master, whatever you do!' Jack begged.

The beating of the drums and the thudding of the feet came closer and closer. The Scarecrow, excited, peered out through the leaves.

'Jack! Look!' he whispered. 'It's astonishing! They're all the same!'

The soldiers, with their bright red coats and white trousers, their black boots and bearskin caps, their muskets all held at the same angle and their brass buckles gleaming, *did* all look the same. There were hundreds of them marching in step, all big and strong and well-fed.

'Magnificent!' exclaimed the Scarecrow.

'Hush!' said Jack desperately.

Ahead of the column of soldiers rode several officers on grey horses, prancing and trotting and curvetting; and behind came a dozen wagons drawn by fine black horses, all gleaming and beautifully groomed.

'What style! What panache! What vigour!' said the Scarecrow.

Jack put his hands over his ears, but the thudding of the soldiers' boots made the very earth shake. Tramp! Tramp! Tramp! Like a great mechanical monster with hundreds of legs, the regiment moved past.

When Jack dared to look, the Scarecrow was standing in the middle of the road, gazing after them with wonder and admiration.

'Jack!' he called. 'Have you ever seen anything so splendid? Tramp, tramp, tramp! And their red coats—and their shiny belts—and their helmets! Oh, that's the life for me, Jack. I'm going to be a soldier!'

'But, master—'

'Off we go! Tramp tramp tramp!'

Swinging his arms briskly, the Scarecrow set off on his wooden legs at such a pace that Jack had to run to keep up.

'Master, please listen to me! Don't be a soldier, I beg you!'

'Remember what the man in the misty cart said, Jack—great fortune! Fame, and glory!'

'Yes, and trouble and danger too—don't forget those!'

'And I'll tell you something else,' added the Scarecrow. 'The regiment is bound to have lots of

food. They're such a fine-looking band of men, I'll bet they eat three times a day. If not four.'

That did it for Jack. At the thought of food, he set off after the regiment as fast as his master, soldiers or no soldiers.

It didn't take them long to catch up, because the soldiers had stopped for their midday meal, and the rich smell of beef stew made poor Jack's mouth water from several hundred yards away.

The Scarecrow strode into the camp and marched up to the cook, who was dishing out stew and potatoes to the soldiers as they stood in a smart line holding out their plates.

'I want to be a soldier,' the Scarecrow announced.

'Get away with you, turnip face!'

'I've got all the qualifications—'

'Go on, scram!'

The Scarecrow was about to lose his temper, so Jack said:

'Excuse me, sir, but who's the officer in charge?'

'Colonel Bombardo, over there,' said the cook, pointing with his ladle. 'At least, he's the commanding officer. It's the sergeant who's in charge.'

'Oh, right,' said Jack. 'I don't suppose I could have a potato?'

'Clear off! Get out of it!'

Nearly howling with hunger, Jack tugged at the Scarecrow's sleeve.

'We have to speak to the officer,' he explained. 'This way, master.'

The colonel was sitting on a canvas chair, trying to read a map upside down.

'Colonel Bombardo, sir,' said Jack, 'my master

Lord Scarecrow wants to join your army. He's a good fighter, and—'

'Lord Scarecrow?' barked the colonel. 'Knew your mother. Damn fine woman. Welcome, Scarecrow. Go and speak to the sergeant over there. He'll sort you out.'

'He knew my mother!' whispered the Scarecrow, awestruck. 'Even *I* didn't know my mother. How clever he is! What a hero!'

The sergeant was a thin little man with a wrinkled face that looked as if it had seen everything there was to see, twice.

'Sergeant,' said Jack, 'this is Lord Scarecrow. Colonel Bombardo sent us over to join the regiment.'

'Lord Scarecrow, eh,' said the sergeant. 'Right, your lordship, before you join the regiment you'll have to pass an examination.'

Jack thought: Thank goodness for that! As soon as they find out what a ninny he is, they'll send us packing. But I'd love some of that stew . . .

The Scarecrow was sitting down already, with a big bass drum in front of him to write on. He looked at the exam paper, took up the pencil at once, and began to cover the page with an energetic scribble.

'What sort of questions are they?' Jack asked.

'Ballistics, navigation, fortification, tactics and strategy,' said the sergeant.

'Oh, good. I don't suppose I could have anything to eat?'

'What d'you think this is? A soup kitchen? This is an army on the march, this is. Who are you, anyway?'

'I'm Lord Scarecrow's personal servant.'

83

'Servant? That's a good'un. Soldiers don't have servants.'

'Colonel Bombardo's got a servant,' said Jack, looking enviously at the colonel, who was sitting with several other officers at a table outside his tent, tucking in to stew and dumplings, while a servant poured wine.

'Well, he's an officer,' said the sergeant. 'If they didn't have servants, they wouldn't be able to put their trousers on, some of 'em.'

'They get a lot to eat,' Jack said.

'Oh, for crying out loud,' said the sergeant, scribbling on a piece of paper. 'Take this chitty to the cook, go on.'

'Thank you! Thank you!' said Jack, and ran back to the cook, just in time to see the last soldier in the queue walking away with a full plate.

The cook inspected the chitty.

'Bad luck,' he said. 'There's none left.'

He showed Jack the empty stewpot. Jack felt tears springing to his eyes, but the cook winked and said:

'None of *that* rubbish, anyway. You duck under here, and I'll give you some proper Catering Corps tucker.'

Jack darted into the wagon in a moment, and was soon sitting down with the cook and his two assistants, eating braised beef *à la bourguignonne*, which was rich and hot and peppery and had little oniony things and big pools of gravy and delicate new potatoes and parsley and mint. Jack felt as if he was in heaven.

He didn't say a word till he'd finished three whole platefuls.

'Thank you!' he said finally. 'Can I take some to

my master?'

'He's lunching with the colonel,' said the cook. 'While you was gobbling that up, we had a message to send over another officer's meal. So you're joining the regiment, then?'

'Well, Lord Scarecrow was taking the exam,' said Jack, 'but I don't think he can have passed it. I better go and see.'

'No hurry,' said the cook. 'They'll be there for a while yet, with their brandy and cigars.'

'Cigars?' said Jack in alarm, thinking of the Scarecrow's straw.

'Don't worry. There's a bucket-wallah to put 'em out if they catch fire to theirselves.'

'The regiment thinks of everything,' Jack said.

'Oh, it's a grand life, being a soldier.'

Jack began to think that maybe it was, after all. He thanked the cooks again, and strolled over to the sergeant, who was trimming his nails with a bayonet.

'How did Lord Scarecrow get on in the exam?' he said.

'He answered all the wrong questions. He doesn't know anything at all.'

'So he won't be able to be a soldier, then?' said Jack, relieved.

'Not a private, no, nor a sergeant, not in a hundred years. He's nowhere near clever enough. He's going to be an officer.'

'*What?*'

'Captain Scarecrow is taking his lunch with his fellow officers. You'll need to find him a horse and polish his boots and wash his uniform and keep him smart, and by the look of him you'll have your work cut out.'

'But he doesn't know how to command soldiers!'

'None of 'em do. That's why they invented sergeants. You better go and get him a uniform. The quartermaster's in that wagon over there.'

Jack explained to the quartermaster that the Scarecrow needed a captain's uniform. The quartermaster laid a set of clothes and boots on the counter.

Jack gathered them up, but the quartermaster said, 'Hold on. He'll need a sword as well if he's an officer. And a proper shako. And a pistol.'

The shako was the tall cap that the officers wore. It had a white plume in it, and a shiny black peak. Jack's heart sank as he staggered over to the officers' table. Once he gets all this on, he'll want to be a soldier for ever, he thought.

'Ah, Jack, my boy!' said the Scarecrow happily as the officers left their table. 'Did you hear the wonderful news? I'm a captain, no less! I did so well in the examination that they made me an officer at once.'

Then he saw what Jack was carrying, and his turnip beamed with an expression of utter delight.

'Is that for me? Is that my uniform? This is the happiest day of my life! I can hardly believe it!'

Jack helped the Scarecrow put on the red coat and the white trousers, and the shiny black boots, and two white belts that went over his shoulders and crossed on his chest, and another belt to hold his trousers up just in case. The poor Scarecrow was transfigured with joy.

'Just let the birds try their tricks now!' he said, waving his sword around. 'I bet no blackbird would dare to eat my brain if he saw me like this!'

'Mind what you're doing with the sword, master,' said Jack. 'It's just for decoration, really. Now you stay here and I'll go and find a horse for you.'

'A *horse?*' said the Scarecrow. He stopped looking joyful and looked nervous instead.

'I'll get you a slow old one,' said Jack.

'He won't want to eat me, will he? I mean, you know . . .' said the Scarecrow, delicately twiddling at the straw poking out of his collar.

'I don't think there's any hay in you, master,' said Jack, 'only straw. You'll just have to show him who's boss. Or her.'

The farrier, who was in charge of the horses, was busy putting some horseshoes on a docile old grey mare called Betsy. He said she'd be just the job for an inexperienced rider.

'Captain Scarecrow's a good fighter,' said Jack. 'He's fought brigands and actors and all sorts. But he hasn't done much riding.'

'Nothing to it. Shake the reins to make her go, pull 'em back to make her stop.'

'What about turning left and right?'

'Leave that to her. *Actors*, did you say?' said the farrier.

'Yes, he fought three of them at once. On a stage.'

'Stone the crows.'

'Yes, he can do that too,' said Jack, leading Betsy over to Captain Scarecrow.

'He's very big,' said the Scarecrow doubtfully, when he saw her.

'He's a she. She's called Betsy. She's all ready to ride. Put your foot in the stirrup—there it is—and I'll lift you up.'

They tried it three times. The first time the Scarecrow went straight over the top and down the other side, landing on his turnip and denting his shako. The second time he managed to stay there, but he was facing the wrong way round. The third time he managed to stay in the saddle, facing the right way, but he'd lost his shako and dropped his sword, and his umbrella had come open in alarm.

'Stay there, master, and I'll pick up the bits and pieces,' said Jack.

He gathered up the sword and the shako, and soon he had the Scarecrow looking very proud and martial. Around them the regiment was striking camp ready to move on, and presently the drums began to beat and the sergeant gave the order to march.

Old Betsy pricked up her ears and began to amble forward.

'Help!' cried the Scarecrow, swaying wildly.

'Look, master,' said Jack, 'I mean Captain, sir, I'm holding the bridle. She won't go any faster while I'm here.'

So they moved along behind the column of marching soldiers and the wagons and the horses, old Betsy

keeping up a steady walk and the Scarecrow hanging on to the saddle with both hands.

Presently he said:

'By the way, where are we going, Jack?'

'Dunno, master. I mean Captain, sir.'

'We're off to fight the Duke of Brunswick!' said another officer, a major, riding up alongside.

'Really?' said the Scarecrow. 'And what sort of bird is he? A great big one, I expect?'

'I expect so, yes,' said the major.

'Has he got a regiment too?' said Jack.

'Oh, dozens.'

'But we're just one!'

'Ah, the King of Sardinia's army is coming to join us.'

'So there's going to be a great big battle?'

'Bound to be.'

'And when are we going to fight them?' said the Scarecrow.

'Don't know. They could attack at any moment. Ambush, you know.'

The major galloped away.

'Jack,' said the Scarecrow. 'This battle . . .'

'Yes?'

'I suppose I might get damaged?'

'Yes. We all might.'

'Could you by any chance find me some spare arms and legs? In case, you know . . .'

'I'll make sure we've got plenty of spare parts, don't you worry, master.'

'And you know, you were quite right about my brain,' the Scarecrow said reassuringly. 'I don't miss it at all.'

And on they marched, towards battle.

Some way behind, Mr Cercorelli had caught up with the astrologer.

'I warn you,' he was saying sternly, 'telling fortunes without a licence can lead to a severe penalty. What do you know of this scarecrow?'

The mystic bowed very deeply, and said in a humble voice, 'I cast his horoscope, your honour, and saw evidence of the deepest villainy. The planetary perfluminations—'

'Don't waste my time with that nonsense, or I'll have you up in front of the magistrate. What did he tell you, and where did he go?'

'He said he was going to Spring Valley, your honour.'

'Did he indeed? And did he set off in that direction?'

'No, your worship. Quite the opposite.'

'Did he say what he was going to do in Spring Valley?'

'Yes, my lord. He said he was going to make a fortune, and then go and take Spring Valley in hand. His very words! Naturally, I was going to report him as soon as I arrived at the nearest police station.'

'Naturally. Here is my card. I expect to hear at once if you see him again, you understand?'

CHAPTER NINE

THE BATTLE

M r Cercorelli wasn't the only person looking for the Scarecrow. High up above the countryside where the Scarecrow and his servant had been wandering, an elderly raven was gliding through the blue sky. She was a hundred years old, but her eyes were as sharp as they'd ever been, and when she saw a group of her cousins perching on a pine tree near a mountain top, she flew down at once.

'Granny!' they said. 'Haven't seen you for fifty years. What have you been up to?'

'Never you mind,' she said. 'What's going on over the other side of the hill? There are cousins of ours flying in from all over the place.'

'The soldiers are coming,' they explained. 'There's going to be a big battle. The red soldiers are going to fight the blue soldiers, and the green soldiers are coming along tomorrow to join in. But how are things over in Spring Valley?'

'Bad,' said Granny Raven. 'And getting worse. Have you seen a scarecrow? A walking one?'

'Funnily enough, we heard a young blackbird complaining about something like that just the other day. Shouldn't be allowed, he said. What d'you want to find him for?'

'None of your business. Where did you meet this blackbird?'

They told her, and she flew away.

*   *   *

That evening, after raiding six farms and commandeering all their food, the regiment camped by the side of a river. On the other side of the river there was a broad green meadow, and it was there that they were going to fight the Duke of Brunswick's army the next day.

While the Scarecrow joined his brother officers in a high-level discussion about tactics and strategy, Jack went to help the cooks prepare the evening meal.

'Is this how you always get food?' said Jack. 'You just take it from the farmers?'

'It's their contribution to maintaining the army,' explained the cook. 'See, if we weren't here to defend them, the Duke of Brunswick would come and take everything from them.'

'So if you didn't take their food, he would?'

'That's it.'

'Oh, I see,' said Jack. 'What are we having for supper?'

They were going to have roast pork, and Jack sat and peeled a mound of potatoes to go with it. When he'd done that, he wandered through the camp and looked at everything.

'How are we going to get across to the battlefield?' he asked one of the gunners, who was polishing a big brass cannon.

'There's a ford,' said the gunner. 'We just hitch up the guns and drive 'em in the water and up the other side. We'll do it after breakfast.'

'Where's the Duke of Brunswick's army now?'

'Oh, they're on their way. Only we got here first, so we got what's called tactical advantage.'

'But if he gets to the meadow before we're across, then *he'll* have tactical advantage.'

'Ah, no, you don't understand,' said the gunner. 'Now clear off, I'm busy.'

So Jack went to look at the river instead. It was wide and muddy, and there might have been a ford, and there might not; because normally where there was a ford you saw a track or a road going down to the river on one side and coming out of it on the other.

He went and asked the farrier.

'No, there's no ford,' said the farrier, lighting his pipe with a glowing coal in a pair of tongs.

'Then how are we going to get across the river?'

'On a bridge. It's top secret. The Sardinians have got this new kind of bridge, movable thing, all the latest engineering. When they come, they'll put this bridge up in a moment—well, about half an hour— and we'll go straight across, form a line of battle, and engage the enemy.'

'Oh, I see. But suppose the Duke of Brunswick decides to fire all his cannons at the bridge while we're crossing it?'

'He wouldn't do that. It's against all the rules of engagement.'

'But supposing—'

'Go on, hop it. Scram. And you keep your trap shut about that bridge. It's top secret, remember.'

Jack decided not to puzzle any more, but to collect some sticks instead, so that he could repair the Scarecrow next day if he needed to.

When it was supper time, he and the other servants had to wait on the officers in their tent. Captain Scarecrow was behaving with great politeness, engaging his neighbours in lively and stimulating conversation, and sipping his wine like a connoisseur. The only thing that went wrong was when the officers took snuff after their meal. The proper way to take it was to put a little pinch on the back of your hand, sniff it briskly up your nose, and try not to sneeze; but the Scarecrow had never come across snuff before, and he sniffed up too much.

Jack could see what was going to happen, and he ran up with a tea towel— but it was too late. With a gigantic explosion, the Scarecrow sneezed so hard that all the buttons popped off his uniform, his umbrella opened in surprise, and bits of straw flew everywhere. Not only that; his turnip itself came loose, and lolled on his neck like a balloon on a stick. If Jack hadn't been there to hold it, it might have come off altogether and rolled right across the table.

As soon as the Scarecrow recovered his wits, he looked at Jack in horror.

'Dear me, what a ghastly experience!' he said. 'Was that the Duke of Brunswick attacking us? There was a terrible explosion, I'm sure of it!'

'Just a touch of gunpowder in the snuff,' said Colonel Bombardo. 'Better than snuff in the gunpowder, what? Cannons'd be sneezing, not firing. Damn poor show.'

Presently the sergeant came in and said it was time for all the officers to go to bed. Jack helped the Scarecrow to their tent.

'It'll be an exciting day tomorrow, Jack!' said the Scarecrow, as Jack tucked him up in the camp bed.

'I'm sure it will, master. I better sew all those buttons on extra tight in case you sniff some gunpowder. Goodnight!'

'Goodnight, Jack. What a good servant you are!'

So they all went to sleep.

When they woke up, there was no sign of the Sardinians, but the Duke of Brunswick's army had turned up during the night and made camp in the meadow across the river. There were lots of them.

'He's got a big army,' said Jack to the cook as they made breakfast.

'It's all show,' said the cook. 'Them big cannons they've got, they're only made of cardboard. Anyway, the Sardinians'll be here soon.'

But the Sardinians didn't show up at all. While the Duke of Brunswick's soldiers lined up their cannons pointing straight across the river, the officers of the Scarecrow's regiment rode up and down, waving their swords and shouting orders. Meanwhile, the sergeant was drilling the troops. He marched them along the riverbank and then made them about-turn and march back the other way. Not many of them fell in.

And while they were doing that, the gunners got their cannons all lined up one behind the other to go across the famous secret bridge that the Sardinians were going to bring. The Duke of Brunswick's soldiers kept looking at them and pointing and laughing.

'They won't be laughing when the Sardinians come,' said the chief gunner.

But there was no sign of the Sardinians. Finally, at about tea time, a messenger came galloping up with some shocking news. Jack was close by, and he heard the sergeant telling Colonel Bombardo all about it.

'Message here from the King of Sardinia, sir,' he said. 'He's changed his mind, and he's joining forces with the Duke of Brunswick.'

'I say! What do you think we should do, Sergeant?'

'Run away, sir.'

'Just what he'll be expecting. Very bad idea, if you ask me. We'll do just the opposite—we'll go across the ford, and before the Duke of Brunswick knows what's hit him, we'll give him a sound thrashing!'

'Very good, sir. This ford, sir—'

'Yes?'

'Where is it, sir?'

'In the river, Sergeant. Right there.'

'Right you are, sir. You're going first, are you, sir, to lead the way?'

'D'you think I should?'

'It's the usual thing, sir.'

'Then *charge*!'

And Colonel Bombardo galloped his horse right off the bank and into the water, and disappeared at once. No-one else moved.

No-one except Jack, that is. He saw the Scarecrow looking in an interested way at the river, where Colonel Bombardo's shako had just floated to the surface; and he ran through all the ranks of soldiers and past the guns and seized hold of

Betsy's bridle.

It was a good thing he did, because at that very moment, there came a terrific volley of firing from the Duke of Brunswick's army across the river, and almost at once there came another volley from the other direction altogether: from behind them.

'It's the Sardinians!' someone said.

And then there were cannons going off all over the place. The regiment was trapped on the riverbank, with the Sardinians behind them and the Duke of Brunswick's army on the other side, and there was no ford at all.

The air was full of gunpowder smoke, and no-one could see anything. Soldiers were shouting and crying and running in all directions; bullets were whizzing through the air from every side; cannonballs were smashing into the tents and the wagons; and the Scarecrow was waving his sword and shouting, 'Charge!'

Luckily, no-one took any notice.

Then a stray cannonball whizzed past Betsy's flanks, giving her a nasty fright and taking some of the Scarecrow's trousers with it.

'Whoah! Help!' cried the Scarecrow.

'It's all right, master, just hold on,' said Jack.

And then a bullet clipped the Scarecrow's head, sending bits of turnip everywhere.

'Charge!' shouted the Scarecrow again, waving his sword so wildly that Jack was worried in case he cut Betsy's head off by mistake; but then another bullet came along and knocked the sword out of his hand with a loud *clang*.

'Now look what you've done!' cried the Scarecrow.

He scrambled down from Betsy's back, and he was about to run straight at the nearest soldiers and join in the fight, when Jack saw him suddenly stop and peer into a bush.

'What is it, master?' he said. 'Look, you can't hang around here—it's dangerous—'

But the Scarecrow took no notice. He was reaching right in among the leaves, and then he very carefully lifted out a nest. Sitting in the nest was a terrified robin.

'This is quite intolerable,' the Scarecrow was saying to her. 'Madam, I offer my apologies on behalf of the regiment. It is no part of a soldier's duty to terrify a mother and her eggs. He owes a duty of care and protection to the weak and defenceless! Sit tight, madam, and I shall remove you at once to a place of safety.'

Tucking the nest into his jacket, the Scarecrow set off. There was a short pause when a stray bullet shot his leg off, and he had to lean on Jack's arm, but slowly they made their way through the battlefield. All around them soldiers in red uniforms were fighting with soldiers in blue uniforms, waving swords, firing pistols and muskets; and then along came some soldiers in green uniforms as well. The thunder of the explosions, and the groans and screams, and the crack of muskets and the whine of bullets and the crackle of flames were appalling, and the things Jack saw going on were so horrible that he just closed his eyes and kept stumbling forward, leading Betsy with one hand and holding the Scarecrow up with the other, until the worst of the noise had faded behind them.

There was a bush close by, and before he did anything else the Scarecrow lifted the nest out of his jacket, with the robin still sitting on it, and placed it gently in among the leaves.

'There you are, madam,' he said politely, 'with the compliments of the regiment.'

Then he fell over.

Jack helped him up again, stuffing back the straw that was coming out all over the place.

'What a battle!' said the Scarecrow. 'Bang, crash, whiz!'

'Look at the state of you,' said Jack. 'You're full of bullet-holes, and you've only got one leg, and part of your turnip's gone. I'm going to have to tidy you up—you're badly wounded.'

'I shouldn't think anyone's more wounded than I am,' said the Scarecrow proudly.

'Not unless they're dead. Sit still.'

Jack took a good strong stick from the bundle of spare parts he'd tied on to Betsy's saddle before the battle began. He slid it inside the remains of the Scarecrow's trouser leg. The Scarecrow sprang up at once.

'Back to the battle!' he said. 'I want to win a medal, Jack, that's my dearest wish. I wouldn't mind losing all my legs and my arms and my head and everything, if only I could have a medal.'

Jack was busy tying the rest of the sticks together to make a raft.

'Well, master,' he said, 'if you turned up at that farm with no legs and no arms and no head and no

101

sense, but with a medal shining on your chest, I don't suppose the broom would be able to resist you.'

'Don't remind me, Jack! My broken heart! In the excitement of battle I'd almost forgotten—oh! Oh! I loved her so much!'

While the Scarecrow was lamenting, Jack gave Betsy a carrot.

'Go on, old girl, you can look after yourself,' he said, and Betsy ambled away and disappeared in the bushes.

'Now, master, you come with me,' Jack went on, finishing the raft, 'because we've got a secret mission. It's very important, so just keep quiet, all right?'

'Ssh!' said the Scarecrow. 'Not a word.'

And Jack pushed the raft out on to the water, and he and the Scarecrow scrambled on board; and a few minutes later, they were floating down the river, with the sound of battle and the cries of the wounded soldiers fading quickly behind them.

CHAPTER TEN

MAROONED

While the Scarecrow and his servant were floating down the river, two important conversations were taking place.

The first one took place on the riverbank, where Mr Cercorelli was talking to the sergeant of the Scarecrow's regiment amid the wreckage of the battlefield.

'The last I seen of him, sir, he was charging into battle like a good'un,' the sergeant told him. 'He made a fine figure of an officer.'

'An officer, you say?'

'Captain Scarecrow was one of the most gallant officers I ever saw. Fearless, you might say. Or else you might say thick as a brick. But he did his duty by the regiment.'

'Did he survive the battle?'

'I couldn't tell you that, sir. I haven't seen him since.'

Mr Cercorelli looked at the devastation all

around them.

'By the way,' he said, 'who won?'

'The Duke of Brunswick, sir, according to the morning paper. Very hard to tell from here. It was the King of Sardinia changing sides at the last minute that did for us.'

The lawyer made a mental note to congratulate his employers. The Buffaloni Corporation had important financial interests in Sardinia; no doubt they had reminded the King about them.

'Mind you,' the sergeant went on, 'we got a return battle next month.'

'Oh, really?'

'Yes, sir. And it'll go different next time, because the King of Naples is coming in with us.'

The lawyer made a mental note to tell his employers that as well.

'If you hear any more of Captain Scarecrow,' he said, 'here is my card. Good day.'

*   *   *

The other conversation took place through a window in a little farmhouse.

'Hey! You!' called Granny Raven, perching among the geraniums in the window box.

An old man and his wife were sitting at the table, wrapping their crockery in newspaper and putting it in a cardboard box. They both looked up in astonishment.

'Here,' said the old man to his wife, 'that's old Carlo's pet, the one what escaped!'

Granny Raven clacked her beak impatiently.

'Yes, that's me,' she said, 'even if you've got it the wrong way round. He was my pet. And I didn't escape, I flew off to find a doctor, only I was too late. Now stop gaping like a pair of flytraps, and pay attention.'

'But you're *talking*!' said the old woman.

'Yes. This is an emergency.'

'Oh,' said the old man, gulping. 'Go on, then.'

'Not long before old Carlo died,' Granny Raven said, 'he asked you both to go over and do something for him. Do you remember what that was?'

'Well, yes,' said the old woman. 'He asked us to sign a piece of paper.'

'And did you?'

'Yes,' said the old man.

'Right,' said Granny Raven. Then she clacked her beak again, and looked at the table. 'What are you doing with that crockery?' she said.

'Packing,' said the old woman. 'Ever since the Buffaloni factory opened, our spring's dried up. We can't live here any more. They're taking everything over, them Buffalonis. It's not like what it used to be. Poor old Carlo's well out of it, I reckon.'

105

'Well, d'you want to fight the Buffalonis, or give in?'

'Give in,' said the old man, and 'Fight 'em,' said the old woman, both at once.

'Two to one,' said Granny Raven, looking at the old man very severely. 'We win. Now listen to me, and do as I say.'

*　　　*　　　*

When Jack woke up, the raft was floating along swiftly, together with lots of broken branches and shattered hen-coops and one or two dead dogs and other bits and pieces. The water was muddy and turbid, and the sun was beating down from a hot sky, and the Scarecrow was sitting placidly watching the distant banks go by.

'Master! Why didn't you wake me up before we drifted this far down the river?'

'Oh, we're making wonderful progress, Jack. You'd never believe how far we've come!'

'I don't think it's taking us to Spring Valley, though,' said Jack, standing up and shading his eyes to look ahead.

Very soon he couldn't even see the banks anymore, and the water, when he dipped his hand in, turned out to be too salty to drink.

'Master,' he said, 'we're drifting out to sea! I think we've left the land altogether!'

The Scarecrow was astonished.

'Just like that?' he said. 'We don't have to pay a toll, or anything? How clever! I never thought I'd go to sea. This will be very interesting.'

'Why, yes, it will, master,' said Jack. 'We don't know whether we'll drown before we starve to

106

death, or starve to death before we drown. Or die of thirst, maybe. It'll be interesting to find out. We'd be better off getting shot to pieces by cannonballs, if you ask me.'

'Now then, you're forgetting the man in the misty cart, Jack! Fame and glory, remember!'

'I think we've had that already, master. We're on to the danger and suffering now.'

'But it ends in triumph and happiness!'

Jack was too fed up to say anything. He sat on the edge of the raft and stared glumly all around. There was not a speck of land anywhere, and the sun glared like a furnace in the burning sky.

The Scarecrow saw his unhappiness, and said, 'Cheer up, Jack! I'm sure that success is just around the corner.'

'We're at sea, master. There aren't any corners.'

'Hmm,' said the Scarecrow. 'I think I'll scan the horizon.'

So Jack held on to his master's legs, and the Scarecrow held on to Jack's head, and peered this way and that, shading his eyes with the umbrella; but there was nothing to be seen except more and more water.

'Very dull,' said the Scarecrow, a little disappointed. 'There isn't even a seagull to scare.'

'I don't like the look of those clouds, though,' said Jack, pointing at the horizon. 'I think we're going to have a storm. Well, this is just what we need, I must say.'

The clouds got higher and bigger and darker as they watched, and presently a stiff wind began to blow, making the water lurch up and down in a very unpleasant way.

'A storm at sea, Jack!' said the Scarecrow eagerly.

'This will be a noble spectacle! All the awe-inspiring powers of nature will be unleashed over our very heads. There—you see?'

There was a flash of lightning, and only a few seconds later, the loudest crash of thunder Jack had ever heard. And then came the rain. The heavy drops hurtled down as fast as bullets, and almost as hard.

'Never mind, my boy,' shouted the Scarecrow over the noise. 'Here—shelter under my umbrella!'

'No, master! Put it down, whatever you do! We'll be struck by lightning, and that'll be the end for both of us!'

The two of them clung together on their fragile raft, with the waves getting higher and rougher, and the sky getting darker, and the thunder getting closer, and the wind getting fiercer every minute.

And then Jack felt the sticks of the raft beginning to come loose.

'Master! Hold on! Don't let go!' he cried.

'This is exciting, Jack! Boom! Crash! Whoosh! Splash!'

Then the biggest wave of all swept over them, and the raft collapsed completely.

'Oh no—it's coming apart—help! Help!'

Jack and the Scarecrow fell into the water, among the loose sticks and bits of string that were all that was left of the raft.

'Master! Help! I can't swim!'

'Don't worry, my boy. I can float. You can hold on to me! I shan't let you down!'

Jack didn't dare open his mouth again in case he swallowed more sea. In mortal terror, he clung to his master as the waves hurled them this way and that.

How long they floated he had no idea. But eventually, the storm passed over; the waves calmed down, the clouds rolled away, and the sun came out. Jack was trembling with the effort of holding tight, and weak from hunger and thirst, and still very frightened, so when the Scarecrow said something, he had to reply:

'What's that, master? I didn't hear you.'

'I said I can see a tree, Jack.'

'What? Where?'

The Scarecrow twisted around a bit in the water and stood up. Jack was too amazed to do more than lie there and look up as his master stood above him, shaking the water out of his clothes and pointing ahead.

Then Jack realized that he wasn't floating any more. In fact, he was lying in very shallow water at the edge of a beach.

'We're safe!' he cried. 'We haven't drowned! We're still alive!'

He jumped to his feet and skipped ashore, full of joy. It didn't matter that he was cold and wet and hungry—nothing like that mattered a bit. He was alive!

The Scarecrow was ahead of him, peering about with great interest. The tree he had seen was a palm tree, with one solitary coconut hanging high up among the leaves, and as Jack found when he joined his master, it was the only tree to be seen.

'We're on a tropical island,' he said. 'We're shipwrecked!'

'Well, Jack,' said the Scarecrow, 'I wonder what we'll find on this island. Quite often people find buried chests full of treasure, you know. I think we should start digging right away.'

'We'd be better off looking for food, master. You can't eat doubloons and pieces of eight.'

The Scarecrow looked all around. It was a very small island indeed; they could see all the way across it, and Jack reckoned that even if he walked very slowly, it would only take him ten minutes to walk all the way round the edge. 'Never despair,' said the Scarecrow. 'I shall think of something.'

Jack thought he'd better look for some water before he died of thirst, so he wandered into the middle of the island, among the bushes, to look for something to drink.

But there was no stream, no pond, nothing. He found some little fruits, and ate one to see if it was juicy; but it was so sour and bitter that he had to spit it out at once, although he thought it was a waste of spit, because he didn't have any to spare. He looked at every different kind of leaf in case there was a cup-shaped one that had kept a drop of dew from the night before; but all the leaves were either flat and floppy or dry and hairy or thin and spiny, and none of them held a single drop of water.

'Oh, dear,' he said to himself, 'we're in big trouble now. This is the biggest trouble we've seen yet. This is a desperate situation, and no mistake.'

With a slow unhappy tread, Jack continued his short walk around the island. Less than five minutes later, he came back to the coconut palm. He tried to climb the trunk, but there were no branches to hold on to; he tried to throw stones at the coconut, but it was too high; he tried to shake the trunk, but it didn't move.

110

He moved into the shade and lay down, feeling so hungry and miserable and frightened that he began to cry. He found himself sobbing and weeping, and he couldn't stop, and he realized that although he was partly crying for himself, he was partly crying for the poor Scarecrow too, because his master wouldn't understand at all when he found his servant lying there dead and turning into a skeleton; he wouldn't know what to do, he'd be so distressed; and with no-one to look after him, he'd just wander about the island for ever until he fell apart.

'Oh, Jack, Jack, my dear boy!' he heard, and he felt a pair of rough wooden arms embracing him. 'Don't distress yourself! Life and hope, you know! Life and hope!'

'I'm sorry, master,' Jack said. 'I'll stop now. Did you have an interesting walk?'

'Oh, yes. I found a bush that looks just like a turkey, and another bush with little flowers the same colour as a starling's egg, and a stone exactly as big as a duck. It's full of interesting things, you know, this island. Oh! And I found a little place that looks just like Spring Valley, in miniature.'

'Spring Valley, master? I'd like to have a look at that.'

'Then follow me!'

The Scarecrow led him to a spot near the middle of the island, where the ground rose up a little way, and some bare rocks stood above the surface. In between them there was a little grassy hollow.

'You see,' said the Scarecrow, 'the farmhouse is *here*, and *there's* the orchard, and *that's* where the vines grow, and the olives are over *there*, and the stream runs down *here* . . .'

111

'Nice-looking place, master. I wish there was a real stream here, though.'

'Then we shall just have to dig a well, Jack. There's bound to be some fresh water under here. That's what we do in Spring Valley.'

'Well . . .' said Jack.

'Yes! A well. You dig there, and I'll dig here,' said the Scarecrow, and he began to scrape vigorously at the ground with a dry stick.

There was nothing better to do, so Jack found a stick too, and scratched and poked and scrabbled at the earth. The sun was hot, and the work made him even thirstier than he was to begin with, and besides, the end of his stick soon got wedged under the corner of a big rock.

He found a stone to jam under the stick so he could lever the rock out. The Scarecrow was happily scratching away further down the miniature Spring Valley, singing to himself, and Jack heaved down on his stick with all his might.

The big rock shifted a bit. He heaved again, and it shifted some more.

It looked a bit funny for a rock. The corner was perfectly square, for one thing, and for another, it wasn't made of rock at all. It was made of wood, and bound with iron. Jack felt his eyes grow wider and wider. The iron was rusty and the wood was decaying, and there was a great big padlock holding it shut, which fell off as soon as he touched it.

Then he lifted the lid.

'Master!' he cried. 'Treasure! Look! You were right!'

The box was packed with coins, jewels, medals, necklaces, bracelets, pendants, rings for ears and rings for fingers, medallions, and every kind of gold ornament. They spilled out of the top of the box and jingled heavily as they fell on the ground. The Scarecrow's muddy little eyes couldn't open wide at the best of times, but they were fairly goggling.

'Well, that's amazing, Jack,' he said.

The Scarecrow picked up an earring and felt around the side of his turnip for an ear, but there wasn't one. Then he picked up a necklace and tried to put it on, but it wouldn't go over his turnip at all; so he put a golden bracelet on his signpost wrist, and it fell straight off. Jack plunged his hands into the chest and filled them with coins and jewels, holding them high and letting them fall down through his fingers.

'We must be millionaires, master!' he said.

But his mouth was so dry that he couldn't speak properly.

'All the same,' he croaked, 'I'd rather have some water.'

'Would you, my boy? There should be enough in the well by now. Come and see.'

Jack thought he was hallucinating. He scrambled to his feet and ran after the Scarecrow, and sure enough, in the spot where he'd been digging, a little stream had started bubbling up.

'Oh, master! Oh, thank you! Oh! Oh! Oh!'

Jack flung himself to the ground and plunged his face into the muddy water, and drank and drank and drank until his belly could hold no more.

The Scarecrow was watching him with quiet satisfaction.

'There you are, you see,' he said. 'We understand water in Spring Valley.'

Jack lay back, bloated, and let the blessed feeling of not being thirsty any more soak him from head to feet.

When he got up, the spring was still bubbling away, and the water was trickling down towards the beach. It didn't look as if it would get there, because most of it sank straight down into the dry earth. The Scarecrow was busy somewhere else—Jack could hear him singing to himself—so, looking carefully at the way the earth sloped and where the rocks were, Jack found another stick and began to dig.

'What are you doing, Jack?' called the Scarecrow.

'I'm making a reservoir, master. What are you doing?'

'Sorting out the treasure,' came the answer.

'Good idea.'

So Jack went on digging until there was a hole as deep as his arm and about the same size across, and he patted the earth smooth and tight all around inside it. Then he scraped a trench in the soil, and led the water from the spring down into his new hole. The Scarecrow came to watch.

'See, master, once the water's in there, all the mud will sink to the bottom, and it'll be nice and clear to drink from,' Jack explained.

'Excellent!' said the Scarecrow. 'A splendid piece of civil engineering, Jack.'

Jack scraped another trench at the other side, for the water to run away once the reservoir was full.

They stood and watched the hole filling up.

'Now come and see what I've done!' said the Scarecrow proudly.

He had made a little grotto with some stones and some mud, and he'd stuck diamonds and pearls and rubies and emeralds all over it with some sticky gum from a bush. He'd made a pretty pattern in the ground with some gold coins, and another pattern with the silver ones, and then he'd made some pretend trees out of bits of stick, and draped the necklaces over them like icicles.

'That's lovely, master,' said Jack.

'And I haven't even begun to study the pictures on the coins yet. Oh, there's endless food for the mind here, Jack!'

'Food . . .'

Jack looked longingly at the coconut palm, but the coconut still hung there high up among the leaves, as if it was mocking him. He tried to put it out of his mind. At least he had something to drink.

So while the Scarecrow worked on his grotto, Jack went down to the beach and walked up and down, looking for a fish to catch. But there wasn't a

116

fish to be seen. He could feel himself going a little crazy from hunger.

'Maybe I could eat one of my toes,' he said to himself. 'I wouldn't really miss it, not a little one. But there wouldn't be enough meat on just one. I'd need a whole foot, or two, maybe.'

He paddled up and down at the edge of the sea, sunk in misery. In the middle of the afternoon he went to the reservoir to have another drink, and the Scarecrow showed him the grotto, with great pride, pointing out all the architectural and decorative effects.

'There, Jack! What d'you think of that? Do you see how I've arranged the stones, with all the light ones here and all the dark ones there? I think I'll go and look for some shells now, to stick round the edge. But Jack—what's the matter, my boy?'

'I'm sorry, master. I've tried not to give in to despair—but I'm starving to death—I think what you're making there must be my burial place, and a very nice one too, but I don't want to starve to death . . . I don't know what to do, master, really I don't . . .'

And poor Jack sank down to the ground, too weak to stand up any longer. In a moment the Scarecrow was kneeling by his side.

'Jack, Jack, what was I thinking of! If that blackbird hadn't stolen my brain, you could have made some pea soup. But as it is, the rest of my head is at your disposal, my dear servant. Cut yourself a slice of my turnip, and feast to your heart's content!'

So Jack struggled up and, not wanting to hurt the Scarecrow's feelings, took his little pocket knife and tried to find a place to cut a slice of his

117

master's turnip. The poor thing was so battered and bruised and dried out that it was scarcely a vegetable any more, and it was as hard as a piece of wood; but Jack managed to find a bit round the back where he could cut a little slice, and he did, and crammed it into his mouth.

'Not all at once, my boy— you'll choke!' said the Scarecrow. 'Nibble, that's the thing to do. And drink plenty of water.'

The turnip was hardly edible at all. It was dry and woody and bitter, and it took so much chewing that every mouthful took five minutes to soften and swallow.

Nevertheless, Jack ate it, and even thought he felt it doing him good.

By the time he'd finished, the Scarecrow had come back with some pretty shells from the beach. They spent an hour or so sorting them out, and then they stuck them on the ceiling of the little grotto. Then they dug a lake around it, and led some water into it from the stream, and that kept them going until sunset, and by then Jack's belly was so empty that he kept on making little moaning sounds, and the Scarecrow offered him another slice of turnip.

But there was hardly anything left to hack. A few bitter shreds were all Jack had for supper. And while he hugged his empty belly and tried to fall asleep, the Scarecrow pottered about in the moonlight, fitting every gem and every gold ornament and every piece of priceless jewellery into the grotto palace until it was perfect, and it glittered over its reflection in the tiny lake, looking fit for the queen of the fairies.

Chapter Eleven

An Invitation

Just before he woke up in the morning, Jack had a dream.

He dreamed he was just lying there on the sand, listening to a conversation in the air above. He couldn't see who was talking, but they had rusty voices, like old barbed wire being pulled through holes in a tin can.

'I'll bet you the small one goes before the day's out,' said one voice.

'I reckon the big one's gone already,' said the other.

'No. He's a monster, and they go on for ever.'

'Thin pickings these days, brother!'

'I heard there was a great battle on the mainland. Feasting for days, my cousin said.'

'All gone when I got there. Bones, nothing but bones.'

'The land's bare, brother. The soldiers move on, and who knows where they go?'

120

'Aye, who knows? Did you hear of the factories they're building in Spring Valley? They're making poisons, brother, poisons for the land. Is that little feller dead yet?'

Jack had been listening in his dream, and all of a sudden, with a horrible shock, he realized that it wasn't a dream at all, and that two vultures were sitting in the palm tree directly above him.

'Go away!' he managed to shout, in a voice almost as hoarse as theirs. 'Go on! Scram!'

His cry awoke the Scarecrow, who leaped up at once.

'Leave this to me, Jack!' he cried. 'This is scarecrow's work!'

And he uttered a bloodcurdling cry, and opened and shut his umbrella several times. The vultures, duly scared, spread their wings and lumbered away.

'My dear servant!' the Scarecrow said, full of compassion, as he turned to Jack. 'How long had those two villains been sitting up there?'

'I dunno, master. I heard them talking and I thought it was a dream. I wish it had been—they said I was almost a goner—Oh, master, ever since we began there's been people talking about eating me, and now the birds are at it too—and *I'm* the one that needs to eat!'

'Have another slice of my head, Jack. As long as I have a turnip on my shoulders, you shall not want for nourishment, dear boy!'

So Jack sawed away and cut himself another little scrap of his master's head, and chewed it hard with lots of water. But the poor Scarecrow was looking a great deal the worse for wear by now; Jack's knife had left deep gouges in the turnip, and the bits that were too tough to cut stuck out like splinters.

While Jack sat there gnawing the bitter root and trying to make it last a bit longer, the Scarecrow went off to inspect the grotto. He had an idea for improving the southern frontage, he said; but he'd only been gone a minute when Jack heard a furious yell.

He struggled to his feet, and hurried to see what was the matter. He found the Scarecrow stamping with fury and shouting:

'You flying fiends! How dare you! I'll bite your beaks off! I'll fill you full of stones! I'll boil you! You vagabonds, you housebreakers! Squatting—*squatting* in our *grotto*! Shoo! Begone!'

'Calm down, master! You'll do yourself a mischief,' said Jack. 'What's going on?'

He got down on his knees and peered into the grotto.

'Blimey!' he said.

For right in the centre there was a nest, and

sitting on the nest was a little speckled bird. As Jack watched, another little bird flew in with a worm and gave it to the one on the nest, and as the one on the nest reached up for the worm, Jack saw

122

that there were four eggs beneath her.

Eggs, thought Jack. *Eggs!*

'Jack?' called the Scarecrow from behind him. 'Be careful—they go for the eyes, these fiends—stand back and let me deal with them!'

The two little speckled birds were looking at Jack. He licked his lips, and swallowed. Then he sighed.

'I suppose,' he said reluctantly, 'you better stay there, since you've got some eggs to look after.'

They said nothing.

'Jack?' said the Scarecrow anxiously.

'It's all right, master,' said Jack, standing up and feeling dizzy, so that he had to hold on to the Scarecrow for a moment. 'They're sitting on some eggs.'

'Eggs, eh?' said the Scarecrow severely. 'Well, that obviously means that hostilities are suspended until they hatch. Very well,' he called, 'you, you birds in there, in view of your impending parenthood, I shall not scare you away. But you must keep the place tidy, and leave as soon as your chicks have flown.'

The male bird flew out and perched on a nearby twig.

'Good morning,' he said. 'And what do you do?'

The Scarecrow blinked, and scratched his turnip.

'Well, I, um—' he began.

'Lord Scarecrow's in the agricultural business,' said Jack.

123

'Jolly good,' said the bird. 'And have you come a long way?'

'All the way from Spring Valley,' said the Scarecrow.

'Splendid. Well done,' said the bird, and flew away.

Now Jack was sure he was hallucinating. As a matter of fact, he didn't feel at all well.

'Jack, my boy,' said the Scarecrow, 'I wonder if I could ask you to adjust my turnip a fraction. I think it's coming loose.'

'Let's go down to the beach, master,' Jack said. 'It's too bright to see here. There's a bit of shade there, under the coconut tree.'

Leaning on his digging stick, Jack made his way through the scrubby bushes with the Scarecrow holding the umbrella over him. It really was almost too hot to bear.

When they reached the coconut tree, they had a surprise, because a flock of pigeons rose out of it noisily, making the leaves wave. And just as the pigeons flew away, the coconut fell on to the sand with a thud.

'Oh! Thank goodness!' cried Jack, and ran to pick it up.

He turned it over and over, feeling the milk sloshing this way and that. He took out his knife and dug a hole in the end, and drank every drop. There wasn't actually as much as he'd thought, and what's more, it was going rancid.

'Jack—my boy—help—'

The Scarecrow was tottering and stumbling over the sand, trying to hold his turnip on. But it had been so bashed and hacked about that it wasn't going to stay on, and besides, as Jack saw when he helped his master to sit down in the shade, the broomstick he'd had for a spine was badly cracked.

'Dear oh dear, master, you're in a worse state than me,' Jack said. 'At least we can do something about you. Lie still, and I'll take your spine out first, and then put my digging stick there instead.'

'Is it a dangerous operation?' said the Scarecrow faintly.

'Nothing to it,' said Jack. 'Just don't wriggle.'

As soon as the new spine was in place, Jack picked up the turnip— but alas! It fell apart entirely.

And now what could he do?

There was only one thing for it.

'Here we go, master,' he said. 'Here's a new head for you.'

He jammed the coconut down on to the end of the digging stick, and at once the Scarecrow sat up.

He turned his new head from side to side, and

brushed the tuft of spiky hair on the top. Oddly enough, the expressions of surprise and delight and pleasure that passed over the coconut were exactly the same as the ones Jack remembered from the turnip. The Scarecrow looked just like himself again; in fact he looked much better than before.

'You look very handsome, master,' said Jack.

'I *feel* handsome! I don't think I've ever felt so handsome. Jack, my boy, you are a wonder. Thank you a thousand times!'

But the wandering about, and the hot sun, and the rancid coconut milk on his empty stomach were all too much for Jack.

'Can I sit under your umbrella for a minute, master?' said Jack. 'I'm feeling ever so hot and dizzy.'

'Of course!'

So they sat side by side for a few minutes. But Jack couldn't keep upright; he kept slipping sideways and leaning on the Scarecrow's chest. His master let him rest there until he fell asleep.

And once again Jack had a dream, and heard voices. This time one of them belonged to the Scarecrow himself, and he was speaking quietly, but with a great deal of force:

'It's just as well for you that my servant is asleep on my breast, because otherwise I'd leap up and scare you in a moment. But I don't want to wake him. You chose your moment well, you scoundrel!'

'No, no, you've got it wrong,' said the other voice, a light and musical voice which seemed to come from a bush nearby. 'I've got a message for you, from the Grand Congress of All the Birds.'

'Grand Congress of All the Birds!' said the Scarecrow, with bottomless scorn. 'I've never heard of it.'

'Your ignorance is legendary,' said the bird.

'Well, thank you. But don't think you can get round me with your flattery. Since I can't move, I suppose I shall have to listen to your preposterous message.'

'Then I shall read it out. *The Eighty-Four Thousand Five Hundred and Seventy-Eighth Grand Congress is hereby convened on Coconut Island, that being the place chosen by Their Majesties the King and Queen of All the Birds. The President and Council send their greetings to Lord Scarecrow, and invite him to attend as principal guest of honour, to receive the thanks of the Congress for his gift of a Royal Palace, and to discuss the matter of Spring Valley, and—*'

'Spring Valley!' cried the Scarecrow. 'What's all

127

this?'

'I haven't finished,' said the bird. '—*To discuss the matter of Spring Valley, and to make common purpose in order to restore the good working of the land, to our mutual benefit*. There,' he concluded. 'That's it.'

'Well, I'm astonished,' said the Scarecrow. 'Spring Valley is a very important place. And if you're going to start deciding what to do about it, I insist that I have the right to speak on the subject.'

'But that's exactly what we're inviting you to do!'

'Well, why didn't you say so? Now, you understand, I shall have to bring my servant with me.'

'Out of the question.'

'What!'

'He is a human being. We birds were meeting in Congress for hundreds of thousands of years before human beings existed, and they have brought us nothing but trouble. You are welcome, as our guest of honour, because we're not scared of you, whereas we're all scared of humans. And—'

The Scarecrow leaped to his feet.

'Not scared of *me*? How dare you not be scared of me! I've got a good mind to make war on the whole kingdom of the birds!'

And he stamped away, waving his arms in a fury.

Jack couldn't keep his eyes closed any longer. He sat up and blinked in the burning sunlight, and the messenger bird flew to another bush a bit further off.

Jack said quickly, 'No, please, listen. Don't let my master's manner put you off. He's highly strung, Lord Scarecrow is, he's got nerves like piano wires. The fact is,' he added quietly, looking around to

128

see the Scarecrow stumping up and down and gesticulating in the distance, 'I don't think he'd manage very well without me. He's a great hero, no doubt about it, but he's as simple as a baby in some ways. Ever since his heart was broken by a broomstick he's been desperate, just desperate. His brain even fell out. I'll see if I can get him to change his mind.'

'Don't be long,' said the bird testily.

Squinting against the glare, Jack stumbled through the bushes and out on to the beach. He fell over three times before the Scarecrow saw him. His master came hurrying over the sand, his anger forgotten.

'Jack! Jack! My boy, are you ill?'

'I think I'm going to croak, master. I think I'm going to kick the bucket. But listen—I have given you good advice, haven't I? What I've said to you made sense, didn't it?'

'The best sense in the world!' said the Scarecrow warmly. 'No sense like it!'

'Then do as I suggest, and say thank you very much to this bird, and go and attend their Grand Congress. And maybe you can get to Spring Valley even if I don't.'

'Without you, my faithful servant?'

'I don't think I'll ever see it, master. I'm done for, that's what I think.'

'I shall never leave your side! And you may tell that crested charlatan so, in no uncertain terms.'

So poor Jack had to haul himself up and stagger back to the bird.

'He says he'd be delighted to accept your invitation,' he said, 'and he sends his compliments to the President and Council.'

'I should think so too,' said the bird.

'Did I . . .' Jack tried to say, but he could hardly get any words out. 'Did I hear you right, or was I dreaming? Those two little speckled birds that made their nest in the grotto—you said they were the King and Queen of all the birds?'

'That is correct.'

'Oh, good,' said Jack.

But he couldn't say anything else, because he felt himself falling sideways, and then he felt nothing at all.

CHAPTER TWELVE

THE GRAND CONGRESS

Jack woke up to find himself lying on his back and gazing up at a bright blue sky. He was lying on something soft and comfortable, so he naturally thought he was dead.

But the angels were making a lot of noise. In fact he wondered why St Peter, or the Holy Ghost, or someone, didn't come along and tell them all to stop quarrelling. They sounded like a lot of squawking birds.

Birds!

He sat up, rubbed his eyes, and looked around.

He was sitting in the middle of the island, a little way from the reservoir and the grotto palace, and under the shade of a bush whose leaves and branches had been woven together over his head. Someone had gone to the trouble of putting a lot of soft leaves down for him to lie on, and right next to him there was a pile of fruits and nuts and berries.

'Food! Thank goodness!' he said, and ate them

all up, feeling much better at once.

And everywhere there were birds: giant eagles wheeling above, herons at the edge of the reservoir, jackdaws strutting up and down, skylarks trilling in the sky, flamingos, robins, seagulls, ibises with long curved beaks, a pelican, and even an ostrich. They were flying, singing, pecking, washing themselves, fluttering their feathers, arguing, clucking, and altogether making so much noise that Jack could hardly think.

But where was the Scarecrow? Jack stood up and shaded his eyes against the brilliant sun, and gazed all around. Near the beach he saw his master's familiar shape striding along stiffly, talking and gesticulating to dozens of birds who were moving along with him.

'Well, I'm blowed,' said Jack to himself, and set off through the bushes to find out more.

'Jack, my boy!' said the Scarecrow, waving cheerfully. 'You've woken up at last! And how are you feeling, my dear servant?'

'Well, I dunno, master,' Jack said, making his way shakily over to where his master was standing.

Although the birds didn't seem afraid of the Scarecrow at all, they flew away when Jack came up, and he and the Scarecrow were able to talk without being overheard.

'I suppose I'm still alive,' Jack went on, 'and my arms and legs are all working, so I reckon I must be all right. But what's going on, master? Where did the birds come from?'

'Ah. What happens is that every ten years, the King and Queen choose somewhere to make a nest, and then they summon all the birds to the Grand Congress. Very simple, you see; primitive, really—suits their childish minds. But they were so pleased with the palace we built for them that they just wouldn't go anywhere else. Oh, and I made them let you stay, and bring you some fruit and nuts and so on. I said I wouldn't accept their gold medal otherwise.'

'They're going to give you a gold medal? That's wonderful, master!'

'Yes, they were thrilled. But look—they're calling everyone together.'

On the topmost branch of a shrub near the grotto palace, a chaffinch was calling loudly. All the other birds stopped what they were doing and flew, or strutted, or waddled, or glided into the space in front of her, and settled down to listen.

'Birds of every degree!' the chaffinch called. 'Waders, swimmers, fliers and walkers! Welcome to the Eighty-Four Thousand Five Hundred and Seventy-Eighth Congress of All the Birds! I call upon our noble President to open the proceedings and welcome our guests.'

An elderly pelican hopped on to a rock and spoke in a deep and sonorous voice.

'I declare this Congress open,' he said. 'We have much urgent and important business to discuss. But our first task is the pleasant one of announcing the winner of our gold medal. We have acclaimed many distinguished laureates in the past, but few whose accomplishments were as varied as those of our guest today. With no regard for his personal safety, he clambered high up a stone wall to restore the fallen chick of Dr and Mrs Owl to his parents' nest. Secondly, ignoring the danger of riot and pursuit, he bravely set free five linnets, six goldfinches, and seven blackbirds from their sordid and miserable captivity. Thirdly, in the midst of a

135

deadly battle, and at great personal risk, he carried the nest of Signora Robin to a place of safety.'

Lots of little birds were gazing in admiration at the Scarecrow, who stood beside Jack with a pleased expression on his coconut.

'And finally, using the utmost resources of his architectural skill, our gold medallist built a palace of jewels for Their Majesties our King and Queen to nest in. I am happy to report the appearance of four chicks this morning. The parents and the chicks are all very well.'

The birds cheered loudly. Several took off and flew around in delight before landing again.

The chaffinch called for silence. All the birds fell still once more, and then he said:

'I now invite Lord Scarecrow to come forward and receive the gold medal, and to say a few words.'

The Scarecrow moved with great dignity between the ranks of watching birds and stood beside the President, while four hummingbirds flew up over the Scarecrow's head and dropped a scarlet ribbon very neatly around his neck. The medal hanging from it gleamed proudly on his tattered chest.

The Scarecrow cleared his throat and began, 'Your Majesties! Mr President! Birds of every kind and degree!'

Everyone fell still. Jack crossed his fingers.

'It gives me great pleasure,' the Scarecrow went on, 'to stand here today and receive this tribute. It is true, in the past we may have had our disagreements; some of your people may have stolen—'

The President coughed disapprovingly and said, 'We don't refer to it as stealing, Lord Scarecrow.

Please confine yourself to general remarks of a friendly nature.'

'Oh, you're trying to censor me, are you?' said the Scarecrow, bristling. 'I must say that's typical. I come here in a spirit of friendship to do you the honour of accepting this paltry bauble, and you treat me like—'

The birds were squawking with indignation and raising their wings and shaking their heads. The President clattered his beak loudly for silence, and said:

'Paltry bauble? How dare you! I never heard such insolence!'

The Scarecrow was about to lose his temper. There was only one thing to be done.

'Excuse me,' Jack called out, 'excuse me, Your Majesties, Mr President, Lord Scarecrow and everyone, I think there's just been a bit of trouble with the translation.'

'But we're all speaking the same language!' protested the President. 'There's no doubt whatsoever about the monstrous and unpardonable insult that this *thing* has just expressed. No doubt at all!'

'*Thing*, sir? *Thing*, did you call me?' cried the Scarecrow, and his umbrella opened and closed in a passion.

'Well, you see, that's just what I mean,' said Jack, carefully making his way through the ranks of the birds. 'Mr President, sir, it's clear to me that you're speaking in different languages. You're talking Bird, which is a rich and noble tongue worthy of the great nation of feathered heroes who speak it, and Lord Scarecrow is talking Coconut, which is a subtle and mysterious language full of wisdom and

137

music. So if you'd let me translate for you—'

'And who are you? You're a human being. What are you doing here?' demanded the President.

'Me, sir? My name is Jack, sir, just a boy, that's right, no more than a lowly servant, sir. But I humbly offer my services, at this most dangerous time in world affairs, in the interests of peace and harmony. So if you'd just let me tell Lord Scarecrow what you're saying, and tell you what *he's* saying, I'm sure this Congress will get on very happily.'

'Hmph,' the President snorted. 'Well, you can begin by saying that unless Lord Scarecrow apologizes for that intolerable insult, we shall have no alternative but to strip him of his gold medal and declare war.'

'Certainly,' said Jack, bowing low.

He turned to the Scarecrow and said, 'Lord Scarecrow, the President offers you his profound apologies, and begs you to regard this little exchange of words as merely a storm in a teacup.'

'Oh, does he?' said the Scarecrow. 'You can tell him in return that I am a proud and free scarecrow, unused to tyranny and the despotic rule of a set of feathered popinjays, and I shall never submit to censorship.'

'Righto, master,' said Jack.

He turned to the President and said, 'Lord Scarecrow presents his most cordial and earnest compliments, and begs the Congress to regard his hasty words of a moment ago as being merely the natural and warm-hearted exuberance of one who has all his life cherished the highest and most passionate regard for all the nation of the birds. He asks me to add that he has never in his whole life

139

received an honour that means as much to him as this gold medal, and he is already the holder of the Order of the Emerald Wurzel, the Beetroot Cup, and the Parsnip Challenge Trophy. What's more, he's a Knight of the Broomstick. But he'd gladly relinquish all those honours in favour of your gold medal, which he intends to wear with a full and grateful heart for the rest of his days.'

'He said all that, did he?' said the President suspiciously.

'It's what they call a compressed language, Coconut,' said Jack.

'Is it. Well, if that is the case, then I am happy to accept his apology,' said the President, bowing stiffly to the Scarecrow.

'He says he offers his most humble apology,' Jack told the Scarecrow.

'It didn't sound like that to me,' said his master. 'In fact—'

'No, he was speaking in Bird.'

'Ah, I see,' said the Scarecrow. 'What an extraordinary language.'

'That's why you need an interpreter, master.'

'Indeed. How lucky that you speak it so fluently! Well, in that case, I am happy to accept his apology.'

And the Scarecrow bowed very stiffly to the President.

Seeing this display of mutual respect, all the birds broke into a storm of singing and shouting and flapping and squawking and chirping and cooing. The Scarecrow responded by beaming widely and bowing in all directions. And thus everyone, for the moment, became the best of friends; but Jack thought that they would probably

need a good interpreter for some time to come.

After the formalities, the Congress moved on to discuss the business of Spring Valley. But the Scarecrow didn't seem able to keep his mind on it. Several birds gave reports on the Buffaloni Corporation's poison factory, and the way they'd diverted the streams, and drained the wells, and dried up the fountains; but all the Scarecrow could do was fidget and scratch and pluck at his clothes.

When they broke for a recess, Jack said, 'Are you all right, master? You look a little out of sorts.'

'I think I'm leaking, my boy,' said the Scarecrow. 'I'm suffering a severe loss of straw.'

Jack had a look.

'It's true, master,' he said. 'Something must have loosened your stuffing. We'll have to get you some more.'

'What are you doing?' said the chaffinch, flying down to look. 'What's going on? What's the matter?'

'Lord Scarecrow's leaking,' Jack explained. 'We've got to find some more stuffing for him.'

'Nothing to it! You leave it to us!' said the chaffinch, and flew away.

'I'll take all this old straw out, master,' said Jack. 'It's been soaked and dried and battered about so much that you could do with a new filling. You'll feel much better for it, you take my word.'

He pulled out handfuls of dusty old straw, bits of twig, scraps of rag, and all the other bits and pieces the Scarecrow was so full of.

'I feel very hollow,' said the Scarecrow. 'I don't like it a bit. I can hear myself echoing.'

'Don't worry, master, we'll soon have you filled up again. Hello! What's this?'

Tucked into the middle of all the straw was a little packet of paper wrapped in oilskin.

'That's my inner conviction,' said the Scarecrow. 'Don't throw that away, whatever you do.'

Jack unwrapped the oilskin. Inside it there was a sheet of paper covered in writing.

'Oh, dear,' said Jack. 'I hoped there'd be a picture. I can't read this, master, can you?'

'Alas, no,' said the Scarecrow. 'I think my education was interrupted.'

By that time, a flock of birds had begun to fly down, each carrying a piece of straw or a twig or a bit of moss, and under the chaffinch's direction they packed them securely in the Scarecrow's inside. Each bird flew in, wove its contribution into the rest, and darted out again.

'They're doing some good stuffing, master,' said Jack. 'I'll put this back now, and then they can finish it off.'

'What's that?' said the chaffinch. 'What have you got there? What is it?'

'It's my inner conviction,' said the Scarecrow.

'What's it say? What's it all about?'

'We don't know,' said Jack. 'We can't read.'

With a loud chirrup of impatience, the chaffinch flew away. The other birds went on packing the Scarecrow, but word had got around, and the President himself came along to have a look. While the little birds flew in and out, the Scarecrow displayed his inner conviction proudly.

'You see, it's bound in oilskin,' he said proudly. 'So all through our adventures, it's been perfectly preserved. I knew it was there,' he added. 'I've been certain of it all my life.'

'Yes, but what does it say, you booby?' demanded the President. 'Are you too silly to know what your own inner conviction is?'

The Scarecrow opened his mouth to protest, but then remembered and looked at Jack for the translation.

But Jack didn't have time to say a word, because a harsh *Caw!* from behind him made him jump, and he turned round to see an elderly raven fly down

143

and land on the grass.

She nodded to the President, who bowed very respectfully back at her.

'Good day, Granny Raven,' he said.

'Well, where is it?' she said. 'This paper from inside the Scarecrow. Come on, let's have a look.'

Jack unfolded it for her, and she put a big claw on it and read it silently.

Then she looked up.

'You, boy,' she said to Jack. 'I want a word with you. Come over here.'

Jack followed her to a quiet spot a little way away.

'I heard about your so-called translating,' she said. 'You're a bright lad, but don't push your luck. Now tell me about the Scarecrow, and don't leave anything out.'

So Jack told her everything that had happened from the moment he heard the Scarecrow calling for help in the muddy field to the moment when he'd fainted from hunger the day before.

'Right,' she said. 'Now, there's going to be big trouble coming, and the Scarecrow's going to need that inner conviction of his more than ever. Fold it up, and put it back inside him, and don't let him lose it.'

'But why, Granny Raven? What's this trouble? And is he going to be in any danger? I mean, he's as brave as a lion, but he's not all there in the head department, if you see what I mean.'

'Not that sort of trouble. Legal trouble. Buffaloni trouble.'

'Well, we can run away!'

'No you can't, not any more. They're on your trail. We've got a couple of days' advantage, so we've got to make the most of it.'

'I don't like the sound of this at all.'

'There's a chance,' said Granny Raven, 'but only if you do exactly as I tell you. And hurry up—we haven't got a moment to lose.'

CHAPTER THIRTEEN

THE ASSIZES

The first thing Granny Raven told them to do was get themselves back to the mainland. This turned out to be quite easy. Some seagulls who lived by the nearest fishing port found a rowing boat that wasn't being used, and they hitched it up to a team of geese, who towed it across to the island in less than a day. Once Jack and his master were on board, the birds towed it back the same way, and that very evening, the two wanderers settled down under a hedge.

'Who knows, Jack,' said the Scarecrow, 'this could be one of our last nights in the open air! We'll be sleeping in our very own farmhouse before long.'

Or jail, Jack thought.

The next thing they had to do was make their way to the town of Bella Fontana, which was the nearest town to Spring Valley. By walking hard, they did it in less than a week. Granny Raven had

had to go elsewhere on urgent business, she said, but she'd see them in the town.

'You know, Jack,' the Scarecrow said as they walked towards the market place, 'I might have been mistaken about these birds. They're very good-hearted, fundamentally. No brains to speak of, but full of good intentions.'

'Now then, master,' said Jack, 'just remember: Granny Raven said she'd meet us by the fountain. And while we're in the town, I think you'd better leave the talking to me. You'll be much more impressive if you keep silent and mysterious.'

'Well, that's exactly what I am,' said the Scarecrow.

On the way, he'd managed to lose his gold medal eleven times and the oilskin package containing his inner conviction sixteen. Jack thought it would be a good idea to put them in a bank, and keep them safe till they were needed. So as soon as they got to the town centre, with its dried-up basin which had once been the municipal fountain, they looked around for the bank.

They were about to go inside when a big black bird flew down and perched on the dusty basin and gave a loud *Caw!*

'Granny Raven!' said Jack. 'Where've you been? We were just going into the bank.'

'I've been busy,' she said. 'What d'you want a bank for?'

The Scarecrow explained: 'We're going to deposit my inner conviction. Don't worry. We know what we're doing.'

'You're luckier than you deserve,' said Granny Raven. 'D'you know what that bank's called? It's the Banco Buffaloni.'

The Scarecrow stared at it in dismay.

'These Buffalonis are everywhere!' he said. 'Well, we can't trust this bank, it's obvious. I shall have to look after my inner conviction myself. Where is it? Where's it gone? Where did I put it?'

'You've got it, master,' said Jack. 'It's safe in your straw. But what do we do now, Granny Raven? And what's going on? There's a lot of people around.'

'It's the Assizes,' she said, 'when the judge comes around judging court cases. He tries all the criminals and judges all the civil cases. There he is now.'

As Jack and the Scarecrow watched, the great doors of the town hall opened and out came an elderly man wearing a long red robe, at the head of a procession of men carrying maces and scrolls. Behind him came several men in black robes, who were the lawyers, and finally came the town clerk in a top hat. Escorted by a procession of policemen in their best uniforms, they crossed the square and went up the steps into the law court.

'Right,' said Granny Raven. 'You go in after them, and get a move on.'

'But what are we going to do in there?'

'You're going to go to court and register the Scarecrow's claim to Spring Valley.'

'An excellent idea, Jack!' said the Scarecrow. 'Let's do it at once.'

And before Jack could hold him back, the Scarecrow set off up the steps and in through the doors, with Granny Raven sitting on his shoulder.

Jack darted up behind him, and found the Scarecrow arguing with an official behind a desk.

'But I demand the right to have my case heard!' the Scarecrow was saying, banging his umbrella on the desk. 'It is an extremely important matter!'

'You're not on my list,' said the official. 'What's your name? Lord Scarecrow? Don't be ridiculous. Go away!'

Jack thought he'd better help. They were in such deep trouble already that they might as well dig a bit deeper.

'Ah, you don't understand,' he said. 'This case is a matter of extreme urgency. It all turns on the ownership of Spring Valley, and it won't take long. If it's not settled, you see, all the water'll dry up. Just like the fountain out there. Stick him on the list, and we can get through it in five minutes, and then all the water in the valley will be safe.'

'Go on!' said a man in the queue for the public seats. 'I'd like to see a scarecrow in court.'

'Yeah, let him go first,' said a woman with a shopping bag. 'He's got a nice face.'

'He's got a face like a coconut!' said the official.

'Well, it *is* a coconut,' the Scarecrow agreed.

'Go on, put him on first,' people were saying. 'It's the only laugh we'll have today.'

'Yes! Let the scarecrow have his case heard!'

'Good luck, scarecrow!'

So the man had no choice. He wrote at the top of the list:

Lord Scarecrow in the case of the ownership of Spring Valley.

No sooner had he done that than the door burst open, and in came a squad of policemen. At the head of them was a lean man in a black silk suit. It was the lawyer, Mr Cercorelli, and he said:

'One moment, if you please. Inspector, arrest this person at once.'

The Scarecrow looked around to see who was going to be arrested, only to find the chief policeman seizing his road sign and trying to put handcuffs on him.

'What are you doing? Let me go! This is an outrage!' he cried.

'Go on, boy,' said Granny Raven quietly to Jack. 'Do your stuff.'

'Oh, excuse me,' said Jack to the lawyer, 'but you can't arrest Lord Scarecrow, being as he's already in the process of going to law.'

'I beg your pardon?'

'It's true, Mr Cercorelli, sir,' said the official,

150

showing him the list of cases to be tried.

The Scarecrow shook off the handcuffs, and dusted himself down with great dignity as a bell rang to summon everyone into the courtroom. Mr Cercorelli withdrew to talk urgently to a group of other lawyers in a huddle by the door. Jack watched them closely, and saw them all leaning over Mr Cercorelli's shoulder to read the name of the Scarecrow's case; but as soon as they read it, they all smiled and nodded with satisfaction.

Oh blimey, he thought.

Then he heard the man at the desk say something, and turned to say, 'I beg your pardon?'

'I said you're in luck,' said the official to Jack. 'This is a very distinguished judge you're up in front of. He's the most learned judge in the whole of the kingdom.'

'What's his name?' said Jack, as the doors opened and the Clerk of the Court called for silence.

'Mr Justice Buffaloni,' said the official.

'*What?*'

But it was too late to withdraw. The crowd behind them was surging and heaving to get in, and Jack saw a lot of whispering and pointing and hurrying in and out of side doors. Soon the courtroom was full to bursting, and the Scarecrow and Jack were crammed behind a table right in the middle, with lawyers to left and right, the judge's bench high up in front of them, and a jury filing into the jury box along the side.

Everyone had to stand up as the judge came in. He bowed to the court, and everyone bowed back to him, and then he sat down.

'I'm getting a bit nervous,' Jack whispered. 'And

Granny Raven's vanished. I don't know what to do.'

'No, no, Jack,' the Scarecrow whispered back. 'Have confidence in the law, my boy! Right is on our side!'

'Silence!' bellowed the Clerk. 'First case. Scarecrow versus the United Benevolent Improvement Society Chemical Works.'

The Scarecrow smiled and nodded his coconut. Jack put his hand up.

'What? What?' said the judge.

'Excuse me, your worship,' said Jack, 'but it's all going a bit fast. Who are these United Benevolent Improving people?'

'Well, if it comes to that,' said the judge, 'who are *you*?'

And he beamed at all the lawyers, and they all slapped their sides and roared with laughter at the judge's sparkling legal wit.

'I'm Lord Scarecrow's legal representative,' said Jack, 'and my client wants to know who these United Improvers are, because we never heard of them till now.'

'If I may explain, my lord,' said Mr Cercorelli,

rising smoothly to his feet. 'I act for the United Benevolent Improvement Society, which is the body that holds a majority shareholding in the company known as the United Benevolent Improvement Chemical and Industrial Company, which is the operating organization that runs the United Benevolent Improvement Chemical Works, which owns and operates several factories situated in Spring Valley for the beneficial exploitation of certain mineral and water rights granted to the United Benevolent Improvement Society, which is a registered charity under the Act of 1772, and acts as a holding company in the case of the United Benevolent Improvement Chemical Works by *tenendas praedictas terras.*'

'There you are,' said the judge to Jack. 'Perfectly clear. Now be quiet while we hear this case and find for the defendant.'

'Oh, right,' said Jack. 'Well, my lord, I'd like to ask Lord Scarecrow to be a witness.'

All the other lawyers went into a huddle. Long words came buzzing out like wasps around a fruit tree. The Scarecrow smiled at everyone in the court, gazing all round with great pride and satisfaction.

Finally Mr Cercorelli said, 'We have no objection, your lordship. He will, of course, be subject to cross-examination.'

'Scarecrow to the witness box!' called the Clerk of the Court.

The Scarecrow stood up and bowed to the judge, to the jury, to the clerk, to the lawyers, and to the public.

'Stop bobbing up and down like a chicken and get into the witness box!' snapped the judge.

'A *chicken*?' said the Scarecrow.

'It's a legal term, master,' said Jack hastily.

'Oh, in that case it's perfectly all right,' said the Scarecrow, and bowed again all round.

The members of the public, watching from the gallery, were enjoying it a great deal. They settled down comfortably as Jack began.

'What is your name?' he said.

The Scarecrow looked puzzled. He scratched his coconut.

'It's Lord Scarecrow,' said Jack helpfully.

'Leading the witness!' called one of the lawyers.

'Strike it from the record,' said the judge. 'You, boy, confine yourself to questions. Don't tell the witness what to say.'

'All right,' said Jack. 'He's called Lord Scarecrow. I'm his servant, by the way.'

'And a very good one!' said the Scarecrow.

'Silence!' called the judge. 'Get on with the examination, boy, and as for you, you scoundrel, hold your tongue.'

The Scarecrow nodded approvingly, and beamed at everyone. The people in the public gallery began to giggle.

'Now then,' said Jack, 'I put it to you, Lord Scarecrow, that this United Benevolent Improvement Society is not the legal owner of Spring Valley.'

'Quite right,' said the Scarecrow.

'Then who is?'

'I am!'

'And can you prove that?'

'I hope so,' said the Scarecrow doubtfully.

The people in the gallery began to laugh.

'Silence in court!' said the judge, and glared

155

furiously. When everyone was quiet again, he said to Jack, 'If you don't get to the point, I shall have you both arrested for wasting the court's time. Has your witness got anything useful to say, or has he not?'

'Oh, indeed he has, your lordship. Let me just ask him again.'

'You can't go on asking him the same question!'

'Just once more. Honest.'

'Once, then.'

'Thank you very much, your lordship. Right. Here goes. Lord Scarecrow, how do you know that you are the owner of Spring Valley?'

'Ah!' said the Scarecrow. 'I've got an inner conviction. I've always had it. In fact I've got it here,' he went on, fumbling in his chest. 'I know it's here somewhere. Yes! Here it is!'

'Yes, that's it,' said Jack. 'Your lordship, members of the jury, ladies and gentlemen, this piece of paper proves beyond any doubt whatsoever that Spring Valley belongs to Lord Scarecrow, and these United Benevolizers are being illegal. I rest my case.'

'But what does it say, you stupid boy?' snapped the judge. 'Get your client to read it out to the court.'

'Well, he's never learned to read, your lordship.'

'Well, *you* read it then!'

'But I never learned to read either. It's a big drawback, and if I'd known then what I know now, I'd have arranged to be born into a rich family and not into a poor one. I'm sure I'd have learned to read then.'

'If you don't know how to read,' demanded the judge, 'how do you know what's on that paper? I

156

warn you, boy, you're in great danger!'

'My lord,' said one of the lawyers, 'all he has to do is hand it to your lordship, and your lordship can read it out for the benefit of the court.'

'Oh, no, you don't,' said Jack at once. 'We want separate verification, according to the principles of *non independentem judgi nogoodi.* So there.'

This was getting more and more difficult. But just then, Jack saw a movement out of the corner of his eye, and looked up at a high window to see Granny Raven making her way in, accompanied by a very nervous-looking blackbird. She made the blackbird sit in the corner of the windowsill, and didn't let him move.

'However,' Jack went on, relieved, 'I think I can see a way out of this legal minefield. I'd like to invite my associate Granny Raven to come and take over this part of the case.'

Granny Raven glided down and perched on the table next to Jack, causing great excitement among the public, and great consternation on the part of the lawyers. They went into a huddle, and then Mr Cercorelli said:

'My lord, it is quite impossible to allow this, on the grounds of *ridiculus birdis pretendibus lawyerorum.'*

But Jack said at once, 'My client is only a poor scarecrow, without a penny to his name. Is the law of the land designed only for the rich? Surely not!

And if, out of the goodness of her heart, this raven—this poor, elderly, shabby, broken-down old bird—offers to represent the Scarecrow, because she is all he can afford, then surely this great court and this noble judge will not deny my client the meagre help that she can bring? Look at the vast wealth, the profound resources, the eminent legal minds ranged against us! Your lordship, members of the jury, ladies and gentlemen of the public—is there no justice to be had in the Assizes of Bella Fontana? Is there no mercy—?'

'All right, all right,' sighed the judge, who could see that everyone in the public gallery was nodding in sympathy. 'Let the bird speak on behalf of the Scarecrow.'

'I should think so too,' said Granny Raven, and then added quietly to Jack, 'Shabby and broken-down, eh? I'll have a word with you later.'

The Scarecrow was watching everything with great interest.

'Well, go on then,' said the judge.

'Right,' said Granny Raven. 'Now pay attention. You, Scarecrow, step down from the witness box. I want to summon two more witnesses before I speak to you again. Mr and Mrs Piccolini, into the witness box.'

Nervously, arm in arm, the elderly couple who'd been packing to leave their cottage came through the courtroom and stepped up into the box.

Once they'd given their names and addresses, Granny Raven said:

'Now tell the court what happened just before your neighbour died.'

'Well, our neighbour, Mr Pandolfo,' said Mrs Piccolini, 'he hadn't been well, poor old man, and

158

when he asked us to step over to his house we thought he was going to ask us to call the doctor. But instead he just asked us to watch him sign a piece of paper, and then to sign it as well. So we did.'

'Did he tell you what was on the paper?'

'No.'

'Would you recognize the paper again?'

'Yes. Mr Pandolfo was drinking some coffee, and he spilled a drop or two on the corner of the paper. So it would have a stain on it.'

Granny Raven turned to Jack and said, 'Go on, open it up.'

Jack opened the oilskin package and held up the paper. As the old woman had said, there was a coffee-stain on the corner. Everyone gasped.

All the lawyers rose to their feet at once, protesting, but Granny Raven clacked her beak so loudly that they all fell still.

'Don't you want to hear what the paper says?' she said. 'Because everybody else does.'

They went into a huddle, and after a minute one of them said, 'We are willing to agree to the letter's being read out by an independent witness.'

'In that case,' said Jack, 'we nominate that lady in the jury box.'

He pointed to an old lady in a blue dress. The Scarecrow stood up and bowed to her, and she looked very flustered and said, 'Well, if you like, I don't mind . . .'

She put on a pair of glasses, and Jack handed her the letter. She quickly skimmed it through, and said, 'Oh, dear. Poor old man!'

Then the old lady read in a clear voice:

'This letter was written by me, Carlo Pandolfo,

159

being of sound mind, but not very well in the legs, and is addressed to whom it may concern.

'As I am the legal owner of Spring Valley, and I can dispose of it however I please, I choose this manner of settling the ownership after I peg out.

'And I particularly want to keep the farm and all the springs and wells and watercourses and ponds and streams and fountains out of the hands of my cousins those rascal Buffalonis because I don't trust any of them and they are a pack of scoundrels every one.

'And I have no wife or children or nieces or nephews.

'And no friends either except Mr and Mrs Piccolini down the hill.

'So I shall make a scarecrow and place him in the three-acre field by the orchard and in him I shall put this letter.

'And this letter shall be my last will and testament.

160

'And I leave Spring Valley with all its buildings and springs and wells and watercourses and ponds and streams and fountains to the said scarecrow and it shall belong to him in perpetuity and I wish him good luck.

'That is all I have to say.

'Carlo Pandolfo.'

When the lady reached the end of the letter, there was a silence.

Then the Scarecrow said, 'Well, I did tell you I had an inner conviction.'

And then there was an uproar. All the lawyers began talking at once and all the people in the public gallery turned to one another and said, 'Did you hear that? Well I never—have you ever heard?—and what about—?'

The Clerk of the Court called for silence, and everyone stopped to see what the judge would say. But it was Granny Raven who spoke.

'There you are,' she said. 'That's the long and the short of it. The will is legal, and properly witnessed, and Spring Valley belongs to the Scarecrow, and we can all—'

'One moment,' said Mr Cercorelli. 'Not so fast. We haven't finished yet.'

CHAPTER FOURTEEN

A SURPRISE WITNESS

And everyone looked at the judge. The look on his face was enough to make Jack feel that all his ribs had come loose and fallen into the pit of his stomach.

'The first witness has yet to be cross-examined,' he said. 'Mr Cercorelli, you may proceed.'

'Thank you, my lord,' said the lawyer.

Jack looked at Granny Raven. What was going to happen now? But he couldn't read any expression on the old bird's face.

The Scarecrow climbed back up into the witness box, smiling all around. Mr Cercorelli smiled back, and the two of them looked like the best of friends.

Then the lawyer began:

'You are the scarecrow mentioned in the letter we have just heard?'

'Oh, yes,' said the Scarecrow.

'You are sure of that?'

'Absolutely sure.'

'No doubt at all?'

'No. None whatsoever. I'm certainly me, and I always have been.'

'Well, Mr Scarecrow, let us examine your claim a little more closely. Let us examine *you* a little more closely!' he said, smiling at everyone again.

The Scarecrow smiled back.

'Let's examine your left hand, for example,' said the lawyer. 'It's a remarkable hand, is it not?'

'Oh, yes. It keeps the rain off!' said the Scarecrow, opening his umbrella, and closing it again quickly when the judge frowned at him.

'And where did you get such a splendid hand?'

'From the market place in the town where I starred in *The Tragical History of Harlequin and Queen Dido*,' said the Scarecrow proudly. 'It was a great performance. First I came on as—'

'I'm sure it was enthralling. But we're talking about your hand. You lost your original hand, did you?'

'Yes. It came off, so my servant got me this one.'

'Splendid, splendid. Now can you show us your right hand?'

The Scarecrow stuck his right hand in the air.

'It looks like a road sign,' said the lawyer. 'Is that what it was?'

'Oh, yes. It points, you see. As soon as my servant got this for me, I became very good at pointing.'

'And why did your servant get you a new right

hand?'

'Because the first one broke off.'

'I see. Thank you. So you have neither of the arms you were—ahem—born with?'

Jack jumped up to protest. He could see where this was leading.

'Your lordship, it doesn't make any difference which bits have been replaced—he's still the same scarecrow!'

'Oh, but it does, your lordship,' said Mr Cercorelli. 'We are seeking to establish how much of the original scarecrow created by Mr Pandolfo still remains. If there is none, then the will is null and void, and the estate of Spring Valley passes to the United Benevolent Improvement Society, according to the principle *absolutem absurditas scaribirdibus landlordum.*'

'Quite right,' said the judge. 'Carry on.'

And in spite of Jack's protests, Mr Cercorelli went through the Scarecrow's whole story, showing how every bit of him had been replaced, including the very straw inside him.

'And so, members of the jury,' he concluded, 'we can see clearly that the scarecrow made by Mr Pandolfo, the scarecrow to whom he intended to leave Spring Valley, no longer exists. Every component particle of him has been scattered to the four winds. There is nothing left. This gentleman in the witness box, so proud of his left hand that keeps the rain off and his right hand that points so well, is no more than a fraud and an impostor.'

'Hey!' said Jack. 'No, no, wait a minute!'

'Silence!' said the judge. 'Members of the jury, you have heard an account of the most shameless

164

attempt at fraud, deception, malfeasance, embezzlement, and theft that it has ever been my misfortune to hear about. Your duty now is very simple. You have to retire to the jury room and make up your minds to do as I tell you. You must find for the defendants, and decide that the United Benevolent Improvement Society are the true owners of Spring Valley. The court will—'

'Hold on,' said a harsh old voice. 'What did that scoundrel say a minute ago? Not so fast, he said. We haven't finished yet.'

Every head turned to look at Granny Raven.

'Everybody listening?' she said. 'I should think so too. We've got three more witnesses to call. It won't take long. The next witness is Mr Giovanni Stracciatelli.'

Jack had never heard of him, and neither had anyone else. The lawyers all huddled together and whispered, but they didn't know what to do, and when Mr Stracciatelli came to the witness box carrying a large leather-bound book, all they could do was watch suspiciously.

'You are Giovanni Stracciatelli?' said Granny Raven.

'I am.'

'And what is your occupation?'

'I am the Commissioner of Registered Charities.'

At once all the lawyers rose to their feet and protested, but Granny Raven's voice was louder than all of them.

'You stop your fuss!' she cawed. '*You* brought up the subject of charities, and *you* claimed that the United Benevolent Improvement Society was a proper charity registered under the Act, so let's have a good look at it. Mr Stracciatelli, would you

165

please read out the names of the trustees of the United Benevolent Improvement Society?'

Mr Stracciatelli put on a pair of glasses and opened his book.

'*Trustees of the United Benevolent Improvement Society*,' he read. '*Luigi Buffaloni, Piero Buffaloni, Federico Buffaloni, Silvio Buffaloni, Giuseppe Buffaloni, and Marcello Buffaloni.*'

Gasps from the public gallery—more protests from the lawyers.

'Thank you, Mr Stracciatelli, you can step down,' said Granny Raven. 'I'd like to remind the court of Mr Pandolfo's opinion concerning the Buffalonis. This is what his letter says: *I particularly want to keep the farm and all the springs and wells and watercourses and ponds and streams and fountains out of the hands of my cousins those rascal Buffalonis because I don't trust any of them and they are a pack of scoundrels every one.*'

Still more protests. The judge was looking very sour indeed.

'Now you may say,' said Granny Raven, 'that Mr Pandolfo was wrong about the Buffalonis. You may claim that every Buffaloni born is a perfect angel. That is all beside the point. The point is that Mr Pandolfo did *not* want his land to go to the Buffalonis, and he *did* want to leave it to the scarecrow.'

'But the scarecrow no longer exists!' shouted Mr Cercorelli. 'I've just proved it!'

'You were concerned with his component

166

particles, not with the whole entity,' said Granny Raven. 'So let us take you at your word, and assume that all that matters is the stuff he's made of. I call our next witness, Mr Bernard Blackbird.'

The blackbird flew down and perched on the witness box. He was very nervous of the Scarecrow, who was watching him closely.

'Name?' said Granny Raven.

'Bernard.'

'Tell the court about your dealings with the Scarecrow.'

'Don't want to.'

Granny Raven clacked her beak, and Bernard squeaked in terror.

'All right! I will! Just let me think. It's all gone dark in me mind.'

'You wake your ideas up, my lad,' said Granny

Raven, 'or you'll be flying home with no feathers. Tell the court what you told me.'

'I'm scared of *him*,' said Bernard, looking at the Scarecrow.

'He won't hurt you. Do as you're told.'

'All right, if I have to. It was on the road somewhere. I was ever so hungry. I seen him coming out of a caravan, and then I seen him banging his head. Mind you, that was a different head. That was a turnip.'

'Never mind what sort of head it was. What was he doing?'

'Banging it. He was whacking hisself on the bonce. Then summing fell out, and him and the little geezer bent down to look at it, and—'

'My brain!' cried the Scarecrow. 'So it was *you*, you scoundrel!'

'Silence!' shouted the judge. 'Witness, carry on.'

'I forgot what I was saying,' whined the blackbird. 'When he shouts at me I get all nervous. I'm highly strung, I can't help it. You shouldn't let him shout like that. It's not fair. I'm only young.'

'Stop complaining,' said Granny Raven. 'What happened next? Something fell out of his head.

What was it?'

'It was a pea. A dried pea.'

'It was my *brain*,' said the Scarecrow passionately.

'Stop him!' cried Bernard, flinching. 'He's gonna hit me! He is! He give me a really cruel look!'

'You'll get worse than that from me,' said Granny Raven. 'Tell the court what you did.'

'Well, I thought he didn't have no more use for it, so I ate it. I was hungry,' he said piteously. 'I hadn't had nothing for days, and when I seen that pea I thought he was just throwing it away. So I come down and pecked it up. I never knew it was important. It didn't taste very nice, either. It was ever so dry.'

'That'll do.'

'It give me a belly-ache.'

'I said that's enough!'

'It might have been poisoned.'

'How dare you!' said the Scarecrow.

'Stop him! Stop him!' cried Bernard, fluttering in terror. 'You seen the look he give me? You heard him? Help! He's going to murder me!'

'That's quite enough,' snapped Granny Raven.

'I need compensation, I do,' said Bernard. 'I need counselling. It's stolen all my youth and happiness away, this has. I'll never be the same. I need therapy.'

'Clear off home and stop whining,' said Granny Raven, 'or I'll give you some therapy that'll sort you out for good.'

Bernard crept along the edge of the witness box, flinching dramatically as he came near the Scarecrow, although the Scarecrow didn't move. Then he flew straight for the open window and vanished.

'Our final witness,' said Granny Raven, with a look of distaste after Bernard, 'is the Scarecrow's personal attendant.'

'What, me?' said Jack.

'Yes, boy, you. Get a move on.'

So Jack went into the witness box. The lawyers were busily objecting, but the judge wearily said, 'Let the boy give evidence. The jury will soon see what rubbish it is.'

Granny Raven said, 'Tell the jury what happened on the island where you were marooned.'

'Oh, right,' said Jack. 'We were left on this island, and there wasn't any food, and I was going to starve to death. So Lord Scarecrow very generously let me eat his head. All of it, except the brain, obviously, being as that was eaten already. So I started to eat it, and bit by bit I ate almost all of it, and it kept me alive. And then that coconut fell down and I stuck it on his neck, and very good he looks too. If it wasn't for Lord Scarecrow's generosity in letting me eat his head, I'd be nothing now but a skeleton.'

'So there, your lordship, members of the jury,' said Granny Raven, 'there is our entire case. The United Benevolent Improvement Society, which is currently running poison factories in Spring Valley, and draining all the wells, is a front organization for the Buffaloni family. Mr Pandolfo wanted to keep Spring Valley out of the hands of the Buffalonis, and leave it to the Scarecrow. The only remaining particles of the original Scarecrow are now indissolubly mingled with those of Bernard the blackbird and Jack the servant; and I shall obtain power of attorney to act for Bernard on behalf of all the birds, since he is a feckless wretch; but we maintain that the kingdom of the birds, together with Jack the servant, are now the true and undisputable owners of Spring Valley, in perpetuity.'

'The jury haven't heard my summing-up yet,' said the judge. 'They can begin by forgetting everything they have just heard. The testimony of the Scarecrow's witnesses is to be disregarded, on the grounds that it is more favourable to the Scarecrow than to the United Benevolent Improvement Society, a charity of the utmost worthiness, whose trustees are gentlemen of the highest honesty and integrity, besides employing a large number of *you*. Ladies and gentlemen of the jury, you know what's good for you—I mean, you know your duty. Go to the jury room, and decide that the Scarecrow should lose this case.'

'No need, our lordship,' said the foreman. 'We've already decided.'

'Excellent! It only remains for me to congratulate the United—'

'No,' said the foreman, 'we reckon the Scarecrow wins.'

'*What?*'

All the lawyers were on their feet at once, protesting loudly, but the foreman of the jury took no notice.

'We don't care about all that,' he said. 'It's common sense. Don't matter if he is all different bits from what he was, he's still the same Scarecrow. Any fool can see that. And we're all fed up with the fountains being dry. So what we decide is this: Spring Valley is to be owned by the birds *and* by the servant *and* by the Scarecrow equally.

172

And that's it. That's the voice of the people.'

A great cheer broke out from the public gallery. The judge called for silence, but no-one took any notice. The lawyers were still arguing, but no-one took any notice of them either.

The Scarecrow and Jack were both lifted on the shoulders of the crowd and carried out to the square. Granny Raven went to perch on the fountain while the Scarecrow made a speech.

'Ladies and gentlemen!' he said. 'I am heartily grateful for your support, and I give you my word of honour that as soon as we have closed the poison factories, we shall let all the springs flow again, so that this fountain will run with fresh water for everyone.'

More cheers from the crowd—but then they all fell silent and looked around. From the town hall a group of men, all wearing expensive clothes and dark glasses and looking stern, were walking towards the Scarecrow.

Jack heard whispers from the crowd.

'Luigi—Piero—Federico—Silvio—Giuseppe—Marcello! It's the whole Buffaloni family . . .'

'Well, master,' said Jack, 'it looks like a fight. Let's run away, quick.'

'Certainly not!' said the Scarecrow, and he faced the Buffalonis boldly, coconut high, umbrella poised, the very model of a people's hero.

The Buffalonis stopped right in front of him, six of them, big rich powerful men in shiny suits. Everyone held their breath.

Then the Buffaloni in the middle said, 'Our congratulations to you, my friend!' and held out his hand to shake.

The Scarecrow shook it warmly, and then all the

other Buffalonis gathered round, slapping him on the back, ruffling his coconut, patting him on the shoulder, shaking his hand, embracing him warmly.

'So we lose a law case!' said the chief Buffaloni. 'It's a big world—there are plenty of other enterprises! Plenty of room in this beautiful world for Buffalonis *and* Scarecrows!'

'Good luck to you, Lord Scarecrow! Our best wishes for all your business ventures!'

'If you ever need our help—just ask!'

'We respect a brave opponent!'

'Buffalonis and Scarecrows are good friends from now on—the best of friends!'

And then a café owner produced some wine, and the Buffalonis and the Scarecrow drank a toast to friendship, and happy laughter filled the square; and presently someone brought out an accordion, and in a moment the whole crowd was singing and dancing and laughing and drinking and throwing flowers, with the Scarecrow at the heart of the celebrations.

Chapter Fifteen

Murder by Termites

They slept that night in the farmhouse in Spring Valley. Jack woke up next morning to hear his master calling.

'Jack! Jack! Help! I don't feel at all well!'

'That's all right, master,' said Jack, hurrying along to help. 'You had too much wine last night. Come for a walk—it'll clear your head.'

'No, it's not my head,' the Scarecrow told him. 'It's my legs and my arms and my back. I've been poisoned. Help!'

And he did look in a bad way, it was perfectly true. Even his coconut had gone pale. When he stood up he fell over, when he lay down he groaned, and he was getting twitches in his arms and legs.

'Twitches, master?'

'Yes, Jack! Dreadful ghastly twitches! It's horrible! It feels as if I'm being eaten alive! Call the doctor at once!'

So Jack ran to the town and called the doctor. The Scarecrow was a celebrity now, thanks to the trial, and the doctor gathered up his bag and hurried along straight away, followed by several onlookers.

They found the Scarecrow twitching badly, and groaning at the top of his voice.

'What is it, Doctor?' said Jack. 'Listen to him! He's in a terrible state! What can it be?'

The doctor took his stethoscope and listened to the Scarecrow's chest.

'Oh, dear me,' he said. 'This is bad. Let me take your temperature.'

'No, no! Don't do that!' protested the Scarecrow. 'If you take my temperature away, I'd be cold all through. As it is, I'm hot *and* cold, both together. Oh, it's horrible! Oh, no-one knows what I'm suffering!'

'What other symptoms are you feeling?'

'Internal conniptions. And a nameless fear.'

'A nameless fear? Dear me, that's not good at all. A fear of what?'

'I don't know! Horses! Eggs! Heights! Oh! Oh! I feel terrible! Help! Help!'

And the Scarecrow leaped all over the room, capering and skipping and prancing like a goat.

'What's he doing, Doctor?' said Jack. 'I've never seen him like this. Is he going to die?'

'He's clearly been bitten by a spider,' explained the doctor. 'Dancing is quite the best cure, all the medical authorities agree.'

The Scarecrow overheard him, and sank to the floor with terror.

'A spider! Oh, no, Doctor, anything but that! I'll go mad with despair!'

'Better keep on dancing then, master,' said Jack.

But the poor Scarecrow couldn't dance another step.

'No, I can't move!' he cried. 'All the strength has drained from my body—my nameless fear is going all the way down to my toes—'

'Let me feel your pulse,' said the doctor.

The Scarecrow held out his left hand. As soon as the doctor took his wrist, the umbrella opened, startling the doctor, who stepped back in alarm.

'Try the other one,' said Jack. 'Here, master, point at something.'

The doctor took his road sign in one hand, and a large silver watch in the other. Jack watched the Scarecrow, and the Scarecrow watched the doctor, and the doctor watched the watch.

After a minute the doctor solemnly declared,

'This patient has no signs of life at all.'

The Scarecrow let out a piercing yell.

'Oh no! I'm dead! Help! Help!'

'You can't be dead yet, master,' said Jack, 'not if you're making a racket like that. Can't you find anything that you can cure, Doctor?'

'Dear me, this is a very bad case, a very poor case indeed. There's only one thing for it,' said the doctor.

'What?' said the Scarecrow and Jack, together.

'I shall have to operate. Lie down on the bed, please.'

The poor Scarecrow was quivering with terror.

'Aren't you going to put him to sleep first?' said Jack.

'Of course I am,' said the doctor. 'My goodness, do you take me for a quack?'

The Scarecrow heard the word *quack* and looked around for the duck, but the doctor took a rubber hammer and knocked him on the coconut. The Scarecrow fell down, stunned.

'Now what?' said Jack.

'Undo his clothing,' said the doctor. 'Then hand me my penknife.'

Everyone gasped, and craned closer to look. Jack unfastened the Scarecrow's coat, and laid bare his shirt, with the straw sticking stiffly out of every gap, and his poor wooden neck sticking out of the top.

His master was lying so still that Jack thought he really must be dead, and before the doctor could do anything, Jack flung himself across the Scarecrow and cried and sobbed.

'Oh, master, don't be dead! Please don't be dead! I don't know what I'd do without you, master! Please don't die!'

He sobbed and howled and clung to the poor old Scarecrow, and nothing would move him. Several of the bystanders began to cry too, and before long the room was filled with weeping and wailing, and every eye was gushing with tears. Even the doctor had to find his handkerchief and blow his nose vigorously.

The birds had heard the news, and a great lament went up from all the fields round about, and the bushes and trees were full of piteous cries:

'The Scarecrow's dying!'

'He's been poisoned!'

'He's been assassinated!'

And the loudest wails of lamentation came from the room in the farmhouse in Spring Valley where the doctor and Jack and all the townsfolk were gathered around the Scarecrow. But they didn't come from the people, they came from the Scarecrow himself, because all the noise had woken him up.

He leaped off the bed and cried:

'Oh! Oh! I'm dying! I'm poisoned! Oh, what a loss to the world! Treachery! Assassination! Murder! Oh, Jack, my dear boy, has he cut me open yet?'

'He was just about to.'

'Oh! Oh! Oh! I feel terrible! I've got conniptions all up and down my spine! I feel as if a million little ghosties were nibbling me! Oh—oh—there goes my leg—I'm falling apart, Jack! Help! Help!'

The Scarecrow was running around the room in terror, and the doctor was running after him trying to hit him with the rubber hammer, to put him to sleep again. Jack was running behind them gathering up all the bits that fell on the floor—

179

some string, a bit of wood from somewhere up his trousers, lots of straw—and everyone else was wailing and sobbing.

Then Jack heard a loud *Caw!* and looked round in relief.

'Granny Raven!' he said. 'Thank goodness you've come back! Lord Scarecrow's been taken ill, and the doctor says—'

'Never mind the doctor,' she said, perching on the windowsill. 'He doesn't need a doctor. What he needs is a carpenter. So I've gone and fetched one. Here he is.'

In came an old man wearing a carpenter's apron and carrying a bag of tools.

'Hold still, Lord Scarecrow,' he said. 'Let's have a look at you.'

'He's my patient!' said the doctor. 'Stand back!'

'I want a second opinion,' cried the Scarecrow. 'Let him look!'

Jack helped the Scarecrow back on to the bed. The carpenter put some glasses on and peered closely at the Scarecrow's legs, and then at the digging stick Jack had put in to replace his spine. He tapped them with a pencil, he felt all round them, he looked all the way up and down the faded road sign.

Then he stood up with a solemn expression. Everyone fell silent.

'In my professional opinion,' said the carpenter, 'this gentleman is suffering from an acute case of woodworm.'

The Scarecrow gave a shriek of horror. Everyone gasped.

'And if I'm not mistaken,' the carpenter went on, 'he's got termites in his stuffing, and an infestation of death-watch beetle in his backbone.'

The Scarecrow looked at Jack in despair, and reached for his hand.

'Can we save him?' Jack said.

'He needs an immediate transplant,' said the carpenter. 'He's got to have a whole new backbone, and he needs his insides cleaning out completely. This is a fresh infestation, mind. It's deeply suspicious. In my professional opinion, all them beetles and insects and woodworms got tipped down his neck yesterday.'

'The Buffalonis!' Jack cried. 'When they all came crowding round to pat him on the back! Assassins! Murderers!'

The Scarecrow was paralysed with terror. All he could do was lie there and whimper.

So Jack ran all through the farm looking for a broomstick, but the only ones he could find were already infested with woodworm, or split down the middle, or soft with dry rot.

He looked for a stick of any kind, but the only ones he could find were too short, or too bent, or too flimsy.

Then he ran back to the Scarecrow, who was lying pale and faint on the bed, twitching and whimpering.

And there were a lot more people in the room. The first visitors had now been joined by several elderly women dressed in black, weeping and wailing and tearing their hair. In those days, every town had a band of professional mourners, and these were the mourners of Bella Fontana. They'd heard about the impending death of Lord Scarecrow, and had come to offer their services. Besides, they'd missed the death of poor old Mr Pandolfo, and they wanted to make amends.

'Ladies,' Jack said, 'I know you mean it for the best, but the thing about scarecrows is that what they really like is jolly songs. You got any jolly songs you can sing?'

'That would be disrespectful!' one of the old ladies said. 'We were always told that when someone was on the brink of death, we had to weep and wail, to remind them of where they were going next.'

'Well, that's very cheerful,' said Jack, 'and I'm sure they all appreciate it no end. But it's different with scarecrows. Songs, dances, jokes and stories, else you all go home.'

'Humph,' said the oldest old lady, but then Jack found a bottle of Mr Pandolfo's best wine, and they all agreed to try singing and dancing, just to see how it went.

'Oh, Jack,' whispered the Scarecrow, 'I'm not long for this world!'

'Well, cheer up, master, it could be worse. You're in your own bed, in your own house, on your own farm, and you might have been stuck in a muddy field or lying in splinters on a battlefield or floating about in the sea getting nibbled by fishes. Here you've got clean sheets, and these nice ladies to sing to you, and people looking high and low for a new backbone. But oh, master, don't die! Oh, oh, oh!'

And poor Jack started to wail and cry again, and flung his arms around the Scarecrow, ignoring the danger of catching woodworm.

And that started the old ladies off again. They'd been singing and dancing to 'Funiculi, Funicula', and 'Papa Piccolino', and they'd just started on 'Volare', but Jack's wails and sobs had them howling and screeching along with him, and then the Scarecrow himself joined in, and there was such a row that they didn't hear the doctor and the carpenter coming back. Only when dozens of birds flew around their heads, and Granny Raven cawed at the top of her voice, did all the crying and howling stop.

'We got a broomstick,' said the carpenter, 'and it's a good 'un. This old raven found it for us, and me and the doctor's going to transplant it right away. Everyone's got to go out of the operating theatre, for reasons of concentration and hygiene. When the operation is over, Lord Scarecrow'll need quiet and rest and recuperation, and until then, keep your fingers crossed.'

So all the townspeople left the room, and the doctor and the carpenter, with Jack's help, detached the old worm-eaten spine and emptied out all the beetle-infested straw, and gently and delicately inserted the new stick that Granny Raven had found, and packed the Scarecrow tightly with handfuls of clean fresh straw from the barn.

'Well,' said the doctor when they'd finished and washed their hands, 'we have done all that medical science can do. Now we have to rely on Mother Nature. Keep the patient warm, and make sure that his dressings are changed twice a day. If all goes well—'

'Jack, my boy,' said a well-known voice behind them, 'I feel a great deal better already! I believe I would like a bowl of soup.'

Chapter Sixteen

Spring Valley

They never managed to get the Buffalonis charged with attempted murder by termites, so the case was never solved; but they didn't have any more trouble from them.

The poison factory was closed down, and re-opened as a mineral water bottling plant. Spring Valley water is famous now; every smart restaurant has it on the menu.

They cleaned up the land and cleared out all the ditches, and re-dug the wells, and opened the clogged-up drains, and now the fountains in the town are splashing good clear water all day and night, and the children play in the paddling pools and the birds wash themselves in the municipal birdbaths. Spring Valley water flows to every house, and all the houses have three kinds of tap: hot, cold, and sparkling.

As for the Scarecrow, he was the happiest of anyone. The broomstick that Granny Raven had found, the one that was transplanted to save his life, turned out to be the very one he'd fallen in love with all that time ago. Her fiancé the rake had left her for a feather duster, and, unhappy and abandoned, she had passed from hand to hand, lamenting the loss of the handsome Scarecrow who had proposed marriage to her. When the two of them found themselves united, their happiness was complete.

The Scarecrow spends all his days wandering around Spring Valley, playing with Jack's children, shooing the greedy birds away from the young

corn, and enjoying the fresh air. But he only shoos
the birds away to a special box of birdseed that he
keeps behind the barn, and what's more, there's
always a nest in his coat pocket. The little birds, the
sparrows and robins, queue up for the honour;
there's a waiting list. The Scarecrow and his
broomstick are as proud of the eggs as if they'd laid
them themselves.

'Jack's children?' I hear you say.

Yes, a few years later, when he was grown up,
Jack got married. His wife is called Rosina, and
their children's names are Giulietta, Roberto, and
Maria. They're all as happy as fleas. Granny Raven
is godmother to the children, and she stands no
nonsense from any of them, and they love her
dearly.

And on winter evenings, as they sit by the fire
with some good soup inside them, and the children
are playing on the hearth and the wind is roaring
round the rooftops, the Scarecrow and his servant
talk about their adventures, and bless the chance
that brought them together. There never was a
servant, Jack is sure, who had such a good master;

and in all the history of the world, the Scarecrow is certain, there never was a scarecrow who had so honest and faithful a servant.